PINCHING LOBSTERS

A NOVEL

DAX SANTI

Pinching Lobsters

eBook ISBN-10: 0984909206
eBook ISBN-13: 978-0-9849092-0-9

Print ISBN-10: 0984909214
Print ISBN-13: 978-0-9849092-1-6

daxsanti.blogspot.com
curlyhairedpeople.com

PINCHING
LOBSTERS

Hi Mom!

Chapter 1

"IT'S GETTING LATE." Danny leaned in to hear Brad's comment over the engines of *The Cubicle*. The churning water behind the boat drowned out their conversation. Mist skipped off the waves and wet their faces at high speed. The bounce was rhythmic.

Danny circled *The Cubicle* around for one last moment with her. The time had come for her to go to dry dock. Today was the last time he would call the ocean his office. He had named his boat, *The Cubicle*, six years ago when he started making payments on her to escape the real cubicle hell that had become his life. Her name reminded him of why he took off the tie. He wanted his office to be the sea. The fresh air of the ocean had soothing advantages.

Just one more moment with her and he would turn for shore. Tomorrow, she would get a for sale sign on her bow.

As dive boats go, *The Cubicle* had proven to be a reliable companion. They had taken daily trips together in search of shipwrecks all over the North Carolina coast. Each day, tourists would carefully step off the dock and onto her deck for a day of exploration at the bottom of the sea.

North Carolina was hard on business that relied on the sun. It didn't have the year-long warmth like Florida, and the winters had become too long. Six years of struggling and he could no longer afford to keep her afloat. There just wasn't enough summer sun to pay the year-round bills.

His father Wayne had refused to help with the first payments. He would bark that dive boats in North Carolina were another "dumb Danny idea." Danny would get the "I told you so eyes" – again. When he had first graduated college, he and his best friend Kenny started a small sailboat rental company. They had accumulated twelve Sunfish sailboats in various colors. The Sunfish was easy to sail, even for a beginner, and would surely provide enough to pay the bills. The long winters had put them out of business after two seasons. Kenny gave up and went to work for his father. Danny refused to give in. Now, at thirty-eight, Danny would again start looking for a new line of work.

His father Wayne skippered a boat as well, but *his* was a fishing boat. *Not Yet* was her name, because he had never quite finished restoring her. Her wooden hull had long since needed a good coat of paint. The *Not Yet* was the exact opposite of *The Cubicle's* clean, sleek, fiberglass hull. Like father like son didn't apply to this family.

No way Danny was going back to the fish-blood-stained deck of the *Not Yet*. As a teenager, his clothes had always smelled of dead fish, as did his hands. He loved the ocean, but not as a hunter. He'd rather dive on a reef or seek out the spooky hull of a sunken ship.

Now was not the time to think of that though. He wanted to spend his last moments with *The Cubicle* thinking about the good times.

"It's getting late," Brad repeated louder. Danny didn't scream back. He just acknowledged him with a nod of the head. He knew what he meant. They needed to pull the boat up onto the trailer, which was more easily done in the light of day.

Danny's girlfriend Stacy, his best friend Kenny, and Kenny's wife Stephanie were at the bow of the boat. They were all there for *The Cubicle's* last voyage, or rather its last voyage with Danny.

Stacy kept looking back to Danny. Lately, she always had a worried look on her face – today, even more so.

Danny headed for land. At the dock, he dropped off Stephanie and Stacy. Kenny jumped out as well. His task was to get Danny's old truck and trailer and back them down the ramp – an important job. Danny's truck was not unlike the *Not Yet*. It too could use some paint, but on the second crank she always started.

As Kenny went for the truck, the ladies stuck around to see what kind of men they had, a joke Stephanie often told.

It wouldn't be a swift exit. It never was when Kenny helped. Kenny backed the truck down the ramp, and once again used too much steering wheel, causing the trailer to turn sideways.

"My bad!" he screamed to Danny. "I got it!" he yelled again, as he pulled forward to straighten out. He put it in reverse, and again the trailer buckled on him. On the third try, he managed to get the trailer down the concrete ramp that led into the water – a bit sideways, but in the water nonetheless.

Danny lowered himself into the water at the back of the boat. His shirt made a bubble with air. He swam around to the front where his feet found ground about waist-deep. The water was cool against the warm sun.

Brad threw down a rope, which Danny caught and then held her as if she were his prize racehorse.

"Alright, take her slow," Danny shouted up to Brad. Brad loved to skipper the boat. These last few months Danny had let him sit in the captain's chair more often. Brad was his neighbor, and part-time second mate when needed. At seventeen, he was already a well-trained man of the sea. He was the young surfer type with long blond hair and baggy sea trunks that revealed a tan line at the waist. Danny knew he was capable of docking the boat. Brad took pride in his knowledge of the water and that was enough for Danny. Brad had become his little brother.

The Cubicle eased forward and bounced a little off the wheels that helped guide her onto the trailer. Kenny got out of the truck and ran back to help guide her on.

"My bad, Danny. The trailer is a little crooked," he said.

"That suit and those office desks are making you rusty," Danny said, picking on him.

"You'll see," he said back to Danny, not meaning it to sting as much as it did. Danny gave him the rope, and they both pulled on the bow hard, trying to get it even with the trailer and guide wheels. "Now?" screamed Brad from above.

"No. She's not straight." Danny walked back a few steps to assess the situation. "Back up and try to come more at an angle this way." He pointed and waved the correct approach.

"Ten four." Brad eased the throttle back into neutral, and then reverse. Water kicked up sand as he backed up in the shallow. He rolled the wheel hard left and waited for Danny's signal.

Danny's arms were raised, and he gave him the all forward. *The Cubicle* eased forward a few feet and then Danny spun his hands hard right. Brad followed, and came in at a better angle to the crooked trailer.

Stephanie and Stacy looked on in amusement. Stephanie shouted, "We haven't got all day, boys!"

Kenny and Danny laughed, but this was serious. If *The Cubicle* was off center, she could jump off the trailer when Brad throttled it to get her on. Concrete wins the battle with fiberglass every time. She also wouldn't sell with a hole in her hull. The bow again bounced on the guide wheels. She looked straight enough, so Danny and Kenny backed away.

"Alright, you look straight," Danny checked again. "When you're ready!"

Brad gripped the throttle hard and then thrust it forward. *The Cubicle* spit water from behind and lurched forward onto the trailer.

She still wasn't straight, and rose high on the left-side guide wheels. The bow bucked, and then veered left toward Kenny and Danny. Brad knew this was not good, and quickly put her in neutral to stop the momentum. Danny and Kenny fell backward as their feet caught on the ground below, arms flailing just above the water. The pointed bow bounced in front of them hard, and then quietly she sank back into the water. *The Cubicle* was having second thoughts about being taken from the sea.

"That was ugly," Danny said, as he wiped water from his eyes.

"You guys!" Stephanie didn't like what she saw, "Should we get someone to help?"

"Sorry, bro. She means well," Kenny whispered to Danny. "No, honey! We got it!" he yelled up to her.

"Let me just straighten the trailer," Danny decided. He shouted to Brad. "Back her up." he motioned with his hands. "I'm gonna straighten the trailer on the ramp."

"My bad, man," Kenny said solemnly.

"Don't sweat it Kenny. You just need some practice." He patted him on the back. Danny walked out of the water and jumped into the truck. The good thing about owning a fifteen-year-old Chevy was that you didn't care if the cracked interior got wet. Two cranks and it started. Danny's bare wet foot pressed the gas and pulled forward until the

truck and trailer were straight. He threw it in reverse, and not to out-
shine Brad, he let the trailer veer a little sideways until straightening
out as it went into the water.

threw it in park, jumped out, ran into the water fast, and tackled
y for the hell of it, water splashing around them.

"They never grow up," Stacy whispered to Stephanie.

Danny surfaced found the rope and then shouted, "Try it again, Brad!"

Again, Brad throttled forward. The bottom of the bow found the guide wheels. They stepped back and pulled hard on the rope.

"Do it!" Danny shouted, and once again *The Cubicle* lurched forward. She jumped up onto the trailer and came to a stop, resting nicely in place.

Danny and Kenny quickly tied her down to keep her from jumping back into the ocean. Brad turned the key and gave a sad look to the ignition. It was the last time he'd do that. He felt *The Cubicle* was partially his. He then jumped down from the bow onto the concrete with the confidence only a teenager has.

"Ahh, to be young again," Kenny watched and admired. Then he screamed, "Shot gun!" and ran to the front of the truck.

Danny tightened the wheel to snug the boat and looked to Brad. "That'll do it." They looked at each other in sadness. No words needed to be spoken. Today was a sad day – a last day.

"Meet you at home, honey!" Danny shouted to Stacy. They got in the truck and paused for a moment. Danny turned to them, "Well, we're still men."

"Barely," Brad rolled his eyes from the back seat.

Danny put the truck in drive, "I need a beer."

"I need two," responded Kenny.

The dented old Chevy rolled them up the ramp and *The Cubicle* was pulled from the sea.

CHAPTER 2

"A TOAST!" KENNY proclaimed, alcohol clearly interrupting his thoughts. Kenny didn't drink like he used to in his twenties, but he was enjoying his new three-beer tolerance.

"I propose a toast to Danny. My greatest . . . longest lasting friend . . . in the world." The lights from underneath the waterline of the pool flickered across his face and seemed to interrupt him. He spun around and demanded all five there at the party join him.

"This will probably embarrass us all," Stephanie whispered to Stacy as they rose from their pool chairs, drinks in hand. "Really, sweetie, remember there is a young person here."

Brad gasped, "Whoa, Mrs. Stephanie, I'm seventeen, *and* I've got my own car."

"Apologies, . . . a young man." Alcohol was on her breath as well. She held up her glass to him and gave him a smile. They gathered around in a circle, arms raised with their drinks.

Brad squeezed in beside Danny. "Wait, let me grab a beer."

"Whoa, Brad," Danny interrupted, "There's a Coke in the cooler." He glanced over the fence to see if Brad's father was looking out the window again. He wasn't.

Kenny proudly spoke again, "Danny has been my friend . . . ever since many years ago . . . when we bonded one day realizing both our names end in n-n-y. That's how it all started." He was clearly moved by this memory, "May you find what you are looking for, my friend." He raised his beer high, "To new beginnings."

"To new beginnings," they all replied, glasses pinging in the moment.

Brad's Coke interrupted as the carbonation was released, "To new beginnings!" he joined in. Danny put his hand on Brad's head and messed his hair up a little. Brad may have been seventeen to his thirty-eight, but Brad was a friend.

"To the good times on *The Cubicle*!" toasted Brad.

"Here, here!" added Kenny, "and a toast to *The Cubicle*. She was a good mate, and she looked after Danny for six years." he put his arm around Danny and kissed him on the cheek, spilling some beer on his shirt, neither one noticing.

"Do you know what you're going to do now, Danny?" questioned Stephanie as she pulled her husband off him and forced his arm around her.

Danny looked over to the left of the pool at the end of his driveway. Fresh from the ocean, still dripping from the sea, sat *The Cubicle*. Named after the office job he didn't have, or want. People on vacation from the inland cities loved the name. Some would return each year and say jokes like they've been transferred to *The Cubicle* for the week. She was a twenty-foot dive boat with a center cover console. She could take out twelve divers and show them a world they had never seen.

Danny loved tourists, because the change in environment always made them giddy like school kids on a field trip. He never tired of making sure everyone's air was on and describing the reef below.

Wilmington, North Carolina, was a great place to dive. They have some of the best wreck dives in the world. The area was a graveyard of countless ships. The water wasn't crystal blue like in the Florida Keys. Its allure was seeing the haunting shadow of a ship emerge, as you pulled yourself down the anchor line in little to no visibility.

No tropical angelfish here. Instead, you would see a five-foot group-er – an intimidating sight to fresh eyes, yet hardly a danger, if you kept your distance. Danny always told his divers, just act as if you belong there and don't swim after them. A grouper doesn't bother humans that don't bother it. He always lowered his voice when he said that to add to their adventure.

Sometimes the visibility in these waters was only few feet, and what you can't see could be very unnerving. Shadows would creep in and out of the darkness. Spielberg's *Jaws* was always somewhere out there –

watching. *The Cubicle* had drained every drop from his bank account, yet he loved her like no other. Six years they had made it together. He returned from his thoughts and put his arm around Stacy.

"I'm still weighing my options. I said I'd give it ten years to make it a success. Thought I'd retire on that boat making sure people's air was on . . . but gas and tourism had other plans, I guess." The disappointment in his voice changed the mood around the pool.

After a moment of no one knowing what to say, Stacy interjected, "Danny's thinking about going back to school."

"Ahh, great," added Kenny, "something he was never good at." The alcohol kept him from seeing his insensitivity to the situation.

"You can't take this man too far inland. Brad, you wanna hear a great Danny story?"

"Yes," Brad quickly answered. He admired Danny and loved hearing stories about how wild he used to be when he was younger.

"Uh, Kenny," Stephanie again interrupted, "are you sure that's a good idea?"

"Come on, Steph," Kenny pleaded. "This is hilarious." He turned to Brad, "It was our first semester at NC State – well after midnight. We had just thrown a house party. There were bodies passed out everywhere. You know, college stuff."

Brad listened on with a grin.

"There were only four of us left standing, and Danny here decided he wanted to go down to Myrtle Beach for a swim; a four-hour drive, mind you."

"Great." Danny looked around, knowing the story, "I'll never live this one down."

Not stopping, Kenny continued, "So four of us; me, Danny, Todd and . . . uhh, what was—"

"Gene!" Danny shouted.

"Right . . . Gene, got in Todd's old hoopty and decided to drive there that night. It was really late. Anyway, Danny was the drunkest so we put him in the back seat."

"Todd didn't drink, so he drove, right honey?" Stephanie interrupted glaring at Kenny.

Confused Kenny took a sip of his beer and said, "Oh yeah, right. Todd didn't drink." He looked back to his wife, and then back to Brad,

"Anyway, we were about thirty minutes into the trip and Danny was gone. Passed out, snoring louder than the radio."

Brad looked at Danny and smiled. Danny smiled back and shrugged his shoulders jokingly.

Kenny continued, "Well, we tried to stay awake, but we too, were falling asleep. So about three hours from the beach, we decided to get a room at the Holiday Inn. We couldn't get Danny up, so we carried him to the room and threw him on the bed – passed out."

Kenny started laughing, but tried to continue telling the story, "So, the next morning, Danny, having slept so well," he gave a look to Danny who was just smiling and shaking his head, "having slept so well, was the first up. He put on his bathing suit, grabbed his towel and his boogie board." Kenny was laughing so hard now, he had trouble finishing the story, "He then goes to the lobby and asks the guy at the desk, which way to the beach?"

They all started laughing. "And then," Kenny finished, "The guy at the counter looked at him with a straight face, pointed out the door and said, 'About three hours that way.'"

Kenny tore away from his wife and fell into Danny laughing and high-fiving him. He looked down at Brad, pointed and repeated, "ABOUT THREE HOURS THAT WAY!"

Brad smiled and looked at them both, "You guys are dorks. Boogie boards? We call them body boards now."

"Ewwwwwwww," erupted Kenny, and he and Danny continued to laugh.

The neighbor's window opened and Brad's mother shouted, "Brad, it's getting late."

"Time for bed, squirt," picked Kenny.

"Yeah, right," Brad replied, but not to be outdone he said, "Maybe tomorrow you guys can take me boogie boarding!" He turned to the ladies and gave them a flirtatious bow, "Good night ladies, always a pleasure to see you."

They replied in unison, "Good night, Brad."

As he ran off, he looked back at Danny, "I'll help you wash off *The Cubicle* tomorrow." He ran by the boat and brushed his hand across her bow.

"Sounds good," Danny shouted back. He kissed Stacy on the cheek.

"Ouch," she said. "I told you, don't kiss me with an unshaven face."

"Oh dear,' Danny whispered. "Hey Kenny, let me show you her
"So, now that she's out of water." He popped Stacy on her under-
...und then the men swayed over to the boat.

...se two women sat back down in their pool chairs. "Boys and their
,' Stephanie announced, as they watched them tinker with the ex-
sed prop.

"Yes, well," Stacy looked at her, "it's time for that boy to grow up."

"Has he said what he'd like to do?"

"No, he has no idea: always changes the subject when I bring it up. I'll be honest with you, Steph, I need a little more than an old rusty boat and a pool."

Stephanie tapped her on the arm and said, "Oh, he'll figure it out."

Stacy sighed, "You're so lucky, Steph," the summer night was beginning to cool, and she pulled her light jacket over her shoulders, "Kenny seems to be doing really well with his company and all."

"With his *dad's* company. Selling boxes is a bore. Ha, don't get me started, and that boy is far from grown up. Look at them, still a couple of misfits." They both laughed. "Gotta love 'em, though. We could have done worse." They sat in silence as they watched their boys.

"All these wires need to be changed," Danny showed Kenny.

"Have you talked to your dad, yet?"

"Nah," Danny replied, "He can't wait to give me the 'I told you so speech.' And honestly, I'm not ready to hear it. He'll probably offer me a spot back on his fishing boat, but Stacy would never allow that. She hates the smell. Hell, I do too. Dad and I don't get along enough, anyway. Just bound by blood. He *doesn't* get me, and I sure as hell don't get him. Stacy thinks he's gone crazy. *Maybe* she's right."

"How is Stacy?" Kenny asked.

"She's good." They both looked back to them, "*I promised her more,* and now it's time to deliver."

"What do you mean?" Danny looked him dead in the eyes. "*This is between me and you.*"

"Right on. My lips are sealed," Kenny promised.

Danny lowered his voice, "I'm gonna ask her to marry me on Friday."

"What!" Kenny whispered, "You little devil. About time. You need me to give you any pointers?"

Danny laughed, "Nah, I got this. I'm gonna take her to *where we* had our first date, to The Fisherman's Shack for dinner.'

"Okay, first date place, right?" Kenny interjected, "She'll app that. What else?"

"Well," Danny continued, "we had lobster that night. You kn how they have those tanks there with the live lobsters in them, so you can pick out which one you want."

"Yeah," Kenny replied, looking a little confused.

"Okay," Danny leaned in, "I've prearranged to put the ring around one of the lobster claws in the tank. We'll walk up to the tank, and when they pull out the lobster, I'll drop the question. Hell, I'm gonna get down on one knee and everything."

Kenny thought about it for a minute, "That's not bad. First date place, and an original idea. Sounds romantic to me."

"And she loves lobster!" Danny almost shouted.

"Shhh, keep it down you drunk," Kenny looked over at the girls and waived.

"You gonna be my best man?" asked Danny.

"Oh, you know it," Kenny toasted and took a big sip. "To marriage; welcome to the team."

CHAPTER 3

IT WAS NOW official. Danny was going to pop the question. He had told his best friend, and now he had to tell the only other person that mattered – Dad.

As he drove his pick-up truck to the pier, he wished Mom were still alive. She was the glue that held him and his father together. It had been five years since cancer stole her, and each passing year he and his father drifted further apart.

It was six p.m., so he knew where his dad was – drinking a cold one at *The Pier's End* with his buddies. That was his dad's hangout. Danny rarely went there, except for the occasional beer celebration, like a birthday. He figured this would count as a celebration, but he didn't want his dad to ruin it. He always had a way of ruining the moment, bringing him down. He was getting bitter in his old age, especially with Mom not being around to set him straight.

Danny parked his truck and started the walk to the end of the pier where The Pier's End was located. It was a cool night, and he enjoyed the greeting the wind gave him. If only his father could do the same. Danny took his time and walked slowly.

He stopped halfway down and peered off the edge. The city's lights were beginning to awaken, as was the nightlife. Some local teenagers were talking loudly near him.

Lucky, he thought, as he looked at them for a moment. *If they only knew what lay ahead.* He'd always heard older people say it and suddenly he realized what they meant. The youth had it made. There they were in the present, not a care in the world, and no bills to pay. Where are we gonna go tonight, was their biggest dilemma. He got *now* what they didn't see. Someone provided for them, took care of them – if they only knew.

The wind smacked his face and brought him back. What was he going to do? When he was their age he thought he would have accomplished everything by the time he was thirty-eight, but here he was, still living paycheck to paycheck. Actually, even that wasn't working now. Time was now a bad word to him. If the Stones' "Time Is on My Side" came on the radio he always changed it, ran from it. He didn't like the thoughts it gave him.

Time came and went and hadn't brought him anything new. Except for Stacy. They had been together four years and she was right, he needed to quit delaying the inevitable. Maybe being married would make him feel like a grown-up. He sure didn't know.

He really needed his father now, but that was a lost cause. Losing Mom had really changed his dad. He wouldn't talk of her, yet Danny knew he always thought of her. She was all he knew. They grew up together. And now he just seemed to be waiting on death. Time.

"Time, you are a bad word," he whispered against the wind.

Danny shook his head and tried to quiet his thoughts. He just gazed at the darkness taking over. Where was *his* light? *His* beacon? He was willing to do it. But what was *it?* He would go there, he just needed direction, but go where? *Damn you, Dad. You're supposed to help with this.* Danny put his hands in his pockets and continued walking down the pier.

The bell on the door announced you to the locals. Paul the bartender was wiping down his bar, just as he always did. Time didn't visit this place except to bring grey hair. The pictures on the walls hadn't changed in . . . well, had never changed since Danny knew them. Countless photos of who caught the biggest fish adorned the walls. Baiting hooks was a way of life around here. There were more black and white photos than there were color. All were taken on this pier.

Danny sometimes, when visiting, would say a word like Google, just to see what kind of confused reaction he would get. Conversations here were of tackle boxes and fishing reels. Danny's scuba talk was also a foreign language.

"Danny!" screamed one of his father's friends from a nearby table. No back in the corner table for them. This was their place. *You* go sit in the back. The same cast of characters sat at the same table. There used to be four of them at the table, but Curtis died last year from old age. Danny used to have to pull up a chair but now Larry would scoot over for him. Thank God Andy always sat by his father. If Danny had to, and their arms mistakenly touched it would be awkward. There was no hugging in this family. Danny's father, Wayne, was old school, beard and all. You would never know they were related unless you looked them both in the eyes, they never sat next to each other to give you that chance.

His father's friends treated Danny as one of them, though. After all, he was blood. Still, it always took a few minutes of silence to break the ice. And one expression always broke it, "Paul! Another pitcher!" Danny gave his father a moment to soak it in that he was here, so he went to the bar to buy a round. When he returned they were ready for conversation – about fishing.

"So, how's the catch?" Danny asked.

"'Bout the same, I guess," Wayne finally spoke, "New Rules on what size, what kind, what color of fish you can catch. Can't clam in the south bay. Did you dry dock that boat?"

"Yes, sir. Pulled her out on Monday," Danny spoke like a child. "She didn't want to get out. Put up a fit."

"Bet you haven't washed her barnacles off yet." Wayne took a drink. His tone was as cold as the beer. His was hand steady and unwavering.

Danny decided not to fight and took a drink himself. Besides, Wayne was right, he hadn't. He put it off. He made a mental note to call Brad for some help tomorrow. The conversation never stayed on them long and Danny turned to his friends, "How you guys making out?"

"Just fine, Danny; we're getting along just fine," Larry took a drink and glared at Wayne. Danny knew Wayne's friends liked him. He pictured them trying to convince Wayne to attempt to get along with his son more when Danny was around. They were good 'ole boys, and believed in family. Not right to fight all the time.

"Your father netted a sting ray yesterday. Big as day," Larry added as some froth fell through his mustache down his beard and back into his beer. He gave Wayne the eyes again.

Wayne grumbled and moved in his seat, "Damn thing nearly tore up my net. Slowed me down for an hour trying to get 'er out. Couldn't keep her either. What cha here for? Today your birthday?"

"No, but I do have some news, actually," Danny moved uncomfortably like he needed to use the bathroom. The seat underneath him squeaked and so did he.

"I'm . . . uh—"

"Well, hurry up boy, before we get too drunk to remember what you said," Wayne snorted.

"Hush, Wayne," Andy finally spoke. He rarely did. "Let the boy have his say."

"Yeah, Wayne, can't you see he's nervous," This was all kind of exciting to Larry. Maybe he was getting tired of all the fish talk, too.

"I'm getting married," Danny threw it out there and then added, "Well, if she says yes." They all laughed.

Larry spoke first, since Wayne didn't seem to want to, "Well, now that is news, and some good news at that, isn't it, Wayne?" They all waited for his response, half-worried about what he might say, because he just stared at his son.

"Paul, . . ." Wayne finally spoke, "a round of whiskey here and a double for my son." Relief came over the table. Larry put a toothpick in his mouth and chewed on it with a smile as he stared at Danny. Andy returned to staring at his beer, which meant he was happy, too.

That's weird, Danny thought. *Not at all expected.*

Larry patted Danny on the back, "Congratulations, Danny. That is just great news."

"Thanks." Danny took a big drink in relief as well.

Larry wanted to hear more. "When are you going to ask her?"

"Tomorrow night." Danny thought he could see a smile underneath his father's beard.

"Got it all planned, do ya?" A giddy Larry added, "How you gonna do it?"

Danny proceeded to tell them about the lobster in the tank. They all decided it was a wonderful idea. Wayne didn't say much, but Danny could tell he was proud. Paul brought a round of whiskey and even took a shot himself. He offered some sound advice to Danny, "Welcome to death row." Then he slammed his shot glass on the table.

"Hear, hear!" was spoken in unison. Larry seemed overly happy about it all, or maybe he was just happy to hear something good for a change, something new.

The Pier's End was a pleasant place to be this night.

CHAPTER 4

THE MORNING OF the big proposal started like any other. Danny went outside by his pool to feel the sun on his face, holding a cup of coffee.

Brad was already there with the net, fishing leaves out of the pool, a job he took very seriously. Brad was here a lot. Danny didn't know Brad's parents well, but assumed there might be some trouble with them, or maybe Brad just liked to hang out with him.

He didn't mind. Brad kept him young. He gave him music that was in now, and told him about Facebook long before others his age knew. He liked to impress Danny when he would sing out some old Led Zeppelin. Danny's generation was old, Brad would tell him, but they had some cool music. Danny never told him Zeppelin was before his time as well.

Danny liked this neighborhood. Even though he was only renting, a house with a pool is a good thing, especially one that comes with a neighbor who kept the pool clean and the chlorine levels just right.

"Morning," Danny said, as he sat down in a chair by the pool. Summer was coming to an end, but today was going to be hot. Danny leaned his head back and took in the warmth.

"Found some frogs in the traps again," Brad said, "Don't worry; I set them free this time."

Not looking away from the sun, Danny just smiled.

"We gonna wash *The Cubicle* today, Danny?"

"Yep."

"You gonna let me take her out afterward?"

"Nope."

"Did you watch that game last night?"

"Yep"

"You awake yet?"

"Nope."

Their conversation always had a rhythm to it. Yes, Danny enjoyed his neighbor's company. Brad got out the last of the leaves and threw the long metal net off to the side. The clambering vibration of metal to concrete bounced off the closed-in fence and hit Danny's ears hard. The youth had zero morning etiquette.

Danny sipped the last of his coffee and then stood up and took a deep breath, "Well, I guess now is as good a time as any. I'll get the soap and scrub brushes."

"Alright, I'll grab the hose," Brad ran around the side of the house.

Danny changed into his work clothes and went to get his tools. Beside the pool was a, well, Danny had never quite figured out what it was. It was sort of a half-garage-half-pool house. Half-garage because you could only fit half the car in, and half-pool house because it housed the water pump for the pool. You could tell whoever built it hadn't worked from plans.

Danny kept it clean. It made him feel like a grown-up, the man of the house. His tools were all hung on the walls. Each tool was outlined in black on the wall so you could easily return it to its proper place when finished. Something Brad had helped him with.

He reached up above the table that held the smaller tools and snatched the scrub brush with the five-foot handle. His shirt knocked something small and metal off the edge of the table. It slipped right between the table and the wall. *Damn.* He tried to reach it, but his arm just wasn't long enough. Then he realized he was holding a five-foot extension pole. He laughed to himself. *Yes, Einstein, use the pole.* It just fit between the wall and table. He blindly pushed the small object around. Whatever it was, it was made of metal, and by using sound to hear it move, he pulled it to within reach.

He knelt down and picked up a compass. He wiped away some cobwebs it had just gathered. He made a mental note to pull out the table and clean up behind it, later.

He remembered this compass. His mother gave it to him. She loved to give cliché gifts. He turned it over and it read, *Never get lost.* Danny smiled at it for a long moment. He looked up and whispered, "I miss you, Mom." Moments like this he hoped there was an afterlife and that his mother was at this moment looking down at her son smiling. He put the compass back on the table and grabbed a marker out of a rusty old can. He then outlined the compass. He smiled and looked up again, "And your husband is an asshole. Sorry for cussing."

He could hear the pressure of the hose come on as water started to thrash the hull of *The Cubicle.*

"Let's go, dude!" shouted Brad.

"Be right there." He stood up and put some soap in the bucket and went back into the light of the sun, squinting as his eyes had to readjust.

"When's the last time you washed her belly? She's covered." The entire bottom of the hull had a green film on it.

"I've been slimed!" Danny said dramatically with an odd voice. Brad just looked at him. Danny asked in disbelief, "Ghostbusters? You've never seen Ghostbusters?"

Brad shook his head, "No one under sixty has!"

"Good one, forgot you still watched Sesame Street. Let me get some soap on her." For the next several minutes they worked in silence. Brad would wet the hull and Danny would scrub soap in with the brush.

"You gonna buy me a pizza tonight for helping?" asked Brad.

Danny remembered there was still one other person left to tell his big news to.

"No can do tonight, got something important to take care of."

"Like what?" Brad stopped and looked at him.

"Like ask Stacy to marry me."

The hose turned off. "You for real?"

"Yeah, man. She's the one."

Brad looked at him with a smile, "'Bout time. But, aren't you too old to get married?"

"Funny."

"No, seriously, that's great. I like Miss Stacy. She's fine, too, boss man."

Danny smiled and looked at Brad, "She's fine?"

"Oh, she's fine, Danny. Probably just wants your social security check, though." Brad squirted Danny with the hose and the cleaning came to an abrupt stop.

Everyone now knew except the most important person. He would pick her up at seven.

CHAPTER 5

DRIVING TO PICK up Stacy, Danny began to feel a presence in himself that was new. This was *all* new to him. He'd never taken anyone to dinner just so he could ask her to marry him. He hated doing it in this old pick-up truck. He looked down at the rips in the seats and the cracks in the dashboard. He mainly kept it to haul *The Cubicle* around when needed. Now that that looked to be over, he decided that he would get a new car, once he got a new job.

This was good, he thought. He laid his elbow up on the door and felt the wind on his arm. He was starting a new life, and what better way to do that than to get married. He was calm and couldn't wipe the smile off his face. He went over his checklist in his head. The champagne is there for the toast. The maître d' seemed to be as excited as Danny when he was told of the part he would need to execute.

Danny had gone earlier in the day and picked out the lobster – a beautiful one. Tied around the rubber band that held the large claw closed awaited a modest diamond ring. The maître d' would keep her in the back until they arrived.

The hardest part was going to be doing this in front of people, but it was his duty as a man to show the world he loved this woman. He smiled as he waited for the light to turn green. She was just a block away. Did she have a clue? Would this be the way she would have wanted him to do it? He felt a panic. *Calm down, everyone goes through this*. A horn behind him alerted him to the green light. Danny took a left and pulled up into her driveway.

Instead of sending her a text as he usually did to alert her that he was there, Danny got out and went to the door.

He hadn't rung her doorbell since they first started dating and smiled as he dried the clamminess off his hands on his pants. She unlocked the door and opened it.

"Hey!" *Did I just shout?* She came out and looked at him funny. "Hey," he said again. *Shit. Panic.* "Uh, how did the . . . um . . ."

"Are you okay?" she looked at him as if she didn't know who he was.

He turned and almost ran to the car, "Your chariot awaits!" he screamed from ahead. He opened the door for her and then shut it behind her once she was in. It creaked with age. She rolled down the window – which took some effort.

"Have you been drinking?"

"No, my lady, just in a good mood. I'm starving!" he ran around the other side, climbed in, and cranked it twice. Embarrassed, he looked over to her, "I'm thinking about getting a new car."

"Ha," she laughed, "That'll be the day."

He leaned over and kissed her, "I figured we'd go to The Shack."

"Sure," she said.

Perfect, she has no idea.

"Table for two," Danny said to the maître d' as they entered. He wiped the sweat off his hands on his pants.

"Of course. Right this way. Would you like to dine outdoors or indoors this evening?" the maître d' asked as he turned to Danny.

"I think a table outside would be nice. Alright with you sweetie?"

"Sure."

"Right this way." *The Fisherman's Shack* was on the pier. They had the best seafood menu in town. The lobsters were fresh off the boat. They were taken outside and given a table with a great view of the setting sun. "Will this do?"

"This is perfect," replied Danny.

"Wonderful," replied the maître d'. "Laura will be your waitress to-night." He laid two menus in front of them, "Oh, and, tonight's special is lobster." He gave Danny another look. Danny thought he might be overdoing it and giving him too many looks.

"Thank you," Danny said. The maître d' left them. "So, how was your day?"

"Ahh, work was crazy. Susan is driving me cuckoo. She is such a kiss-up."

Danny needed to change the subject and fast. This needed to be ro-mantic, "Wow, the clouds look great."

Stacy laughed, "I was just thinking the same thing. This is nice for a change. Thanks, Dan." *Perfect,* he thought. *Perfect.*

The waitress approached. She too was looking at Danny with a smile, "Hi folks, my name is Laura. Can I get some drinks started for you?"

Danny looked over to Stacy, "Pinot?"

"Absolutely."

"We'll have a couple glasses of your house Pinot."

"Great and our special tonight is lobster," she looked again at Dan-ny. The overacting in this joint was killing him. "Would you like a few more minutes to look at the menu?"

"Nope, lobster sounds great," Stacy said and she gave her back the menu.

Danny looked at the waitress, "She loves lobster. I'll have the fried clams with some extra tartar please."

"Great." she took Danny's menu as well. She looked at Stacy. "Tony up front will help you pick out your lobster when you're ready."

"Great. Thanks."

By the front door was a large fish tank holding assorted resplendent lobsters. Danny knew Stacy loved this place mainly because you get to pick out your own. Tony the maître d' was waiting for them as they walked up.

The glass couldn't have been cleaner. Danny could tell they had just given it a good wipe. He now prayed she would see it and that another lobster wouldn't cover his. The sparkle hit his eyes. It wasn't the biggest sparkle but it was shining nevertheless – right in their eyes. He could see Stacy written on the back of the lobster's shell. A suggestion the maître d' had made earlier. Stacy's lobster was right there waiting for her to realize the big moment. She leaned in closer to the tank. "Ummmm . . . "

Danny saw her face change. There was no doubt what she was looking at. She was frozen, unable to speak. After a long moment she stood up and looked at him, "Danny," the tone in her voice was unreadable.

Without hesitation Danny did what millions have done before him. He dropped to one knee. The maître d' pulled out the lobster and cut the string that bound the diamond. He wiped it off and handed it to Danny. He then handed Stacy's lobster to the awaiting chef, like a priest would do when giving away communion bread. The chef received Stacy's lobster and returned to the kitchen. The staff had gathered around and with the arriving guests waiting to be seated, the area was full.

Danny took a deep breath, "Miss Stacy Lynn Thomas . . . will you marry me?" he held out the ring, ready for it to be received.

She didn't take it. Again she said, "Danny . . ."

A hush entered the room uninvited. Danny went blank. The silence overwhelmed all except for a woman's voice at the door, "Oh, dear."

Danny's face turned red. Red like boiled lobster. He couldn't think straight. All these people were watching. How could he have been so stupid?

Stacy again said the wrong thing, "Danny, can we go somewhere and talk. It's just the timing . . . I've been . . ."

Danny realized he was still on bended knee. He jumped to his feet. What the hell to do now? One thought kept telling him to run . . . run – so he did.

He turned for the front door, but it was blocked by rubberneckers scrutinizing him. Everyone was just staring. *Wake up* he thought, but relief didn't come. Her voice did.

"Danny, please . . ." she came up behind him.

Again he turned and ran right past her. He needed out of here and fast. He couldn't run through the dining room. There were many more sets of eyes out there, watching the train wreck. He saw the bright lights of the kitchen call to him like the creator himself. *Here my son, come here.* He ran past the entire kitchen staff who had come out to see the event as well. He pushed the swinging door open at full sprint.

All kitchens have a back door for deliveries. There has to be one. He ran past a cooler, past the salad station, past the boiling pots of water, and then he stopped and looked back. There she was, Stacy's lobster. Alive. Waiting to be put in the boiling water. He suddenly felt a kinship with her. He too was about to be boiled. He wasn't thinking straight. He looked around. There was no one there. They were all out there, staring.

Without thinking he snatched Stacy's lobster from the counter. Together they escaped. Together they would be free.

Danny and a flailing shellfish exited through the back door and out of that hot kitchen.

CHAPTER 6

"BITCH, BITCH, BITCH!" Danny pounded on the steering wheel as he sped down the road, "WHY!" Anger pushed aside embarrassment. He turned to the lobster that lay still in the passenger seat, "She always gave me hints to ask her! Always hinted at what she wanted. And what do I get? A 'DANNY WE NEED TO TALK.' FUCK YOU, WE NEED TO TALK!" Again he addressed the lobster, "I bet they're all having a good laugh back there. Some story they'll have to tell. Let me tell you about this dumbass I saw tonight. I WAS DOWN ON MY KNEES!" he shouted to the lobster.

He drove into a corner really hard and the wheels screamed out. The truck jerked back straight. He eased off the gas.

He turned to the lobster, "Don't worry. I'm gonna—" but she wasn't there. "No!" he screamed. He stopped, dead, right in the middle of the road, threw it in park and opened the door. "No, no, no," he was saying to himself as he ran around to the other side and opened the door. There she was, upside down between the seat and the floor, eight legs grabbing at air in an unknown world. He frowned and gently picked her up.

"I got you," he whispered, "I got you, don't you worry, I'm gonna take care of you."

He shut the door and walked around to the other side. He again laid her in the passenger seat. This time, gently. He looked around to see if there were any eyes watching him. He took a deep breath and put it in drive.

"Oh, God . . ." It dawned on him as he ran his fingers through his hair, "How am I going tell Dad?" It was more a statement than a question. He just shook his head and drove off – with Stacy's lobster.

With the sun down, Danny had trouble finding his flashlight in the garage/pool shed. He located it at the back of the table and hoped the batteries still worked. He hit the switch and the beam broke the darkness. It lit up the table, and flashed on the compass. *Don't get lost.* He wasn't sure where he was at the moment, but lost wasn't the word he'd use.

Now where was it? He knew he had put one in here when he'd first moved in. *It must be under the table here somewhere. Ahh, there it is.* A twenty-gallon fish tank revealed itself. *Not the Atlantic Ocean but it'd do for now.* Danny headed inside the house with the tank under his arm.

He needed to wash it out, but Stacy's lobster was currently occupying the sink. Where could he put her? He decided she would be okay on the floor so he picked her up by her back and placed her gently down. She scurried to a corner.

There it was again. His cell phone was buzzing, intruding on his peaceful moment with his lobster. He pulled it out of his pocket. The screen lit up the dark room. He had kept the lights off in case she drove by. He even parked down the street so his car wouldn't reveal his location. He wasn't acting normal. He had just walked two blocks with a bucket of seawater. No easy feat and he'd spilled a third of it.

It was *her.* She had called four times since his escape. He couldn't deal with her right now. Every time he thought of her all he could see were hundreds of eyes looking over her shoulder, staring.

Earlier, he had put his phone on vibrate to keep the noise from screaming at him. For some reason he wanted to know when she was calling. He needed to know. There was some comfort in that. She was all he had known for the last few years. That's what made this all too crazy. It was over. How could they even have a conversation now? It was too much to deal with. He completely shut down the phone and looked down to his new friend.

"I promise as soon as I get you in this tank I'll take off those rubber bands." *The terror it must be for you to have a giant creature like me so easily block your only line of defense with a couple of rubber bands.* He felt the cruelty of humanity, of nature. *If you're inventing something from nothing, why even invent Predators?* He got back to work. He wanted to make the lobster feel as comfortable as he could.

Water spilled everywhere as he tried to rinse out the fish tank. He would swirl water and then flip it, swirl and then flip. It was too big for his modest sink. He kept glancing at her to make sure she didn't disappear again. She just sat there. He felt like she was watching him. When he was finished he wiped the tank clean and set it on the floor. He grabbed the bucket of seawater that was outside the front door. Before closing the door he looked around to make sure no eyes were looking at him.

Back inside he carefully poured the little sea water he had gathered from the ocean into the tank. It filled less than a fourth of the tank but would have to do for now.

"What do you think?" he asked the lobster. Had he lost it? He was talking to a lobster. He didn't care. There was a connection between them now. Danny felt obligated to take care of her. She had been two minutes away from boiling water. Again he pulled out his phone and turned it back on. This time to take a picture of her, or maybe he wanted to see if she had called again. Whatever.

The lobster sat still like a good subject. Danny clicked the photo and then checked to see if it had been in focus. Her black eyes penetrated the screen. What a beautiful creature he thought. *Don't worry, you're safe now.* He laid the phone down on the counter.

He pulled some scissors out of the kitchen drawer and walked over to her. She did not like this, but was already up against the wall. Her shell paused as she prepared to fight.

"Relax," Danny said. "I'm gonna cut these off, okay?" He sat and marveled at her for a moment. He had never looked at a lobster before without wanting to eat it. That seemed repulsive to him now. She was a beautiful creature, protected by a speckled hard shell. She had a large claw on her left and smaller one on her right. They were mighty and almost as big as her entire body. Upon closer observation the claws seemed to have teeth, especially the large one. They were enamel in color and looked like molars. The smaller claw had lots of smaller sharp ones. She was brown but seemed to have this outlining red glow. And she was freckled. Her eight legs were spider-like and confused in this alien environment. Two long tentacles protruded from under her eyes. He wondered what she used them for. And her eyes were on the ends of stems. It was amazing. He wondered about her vision. Then he thought about the boiling water and the fate that so many lobsters ended up in. The pain. Burning eyes.

Her majestic tail lay curled under her. Afraid. He wanted to turn her over, but he could tell she was scared, and he didn't like that.

What was it like to live at the bottom of the ocean? She was lucky. He wanted to return with her there now. Hide under a rock.

He made a mental note to google lobsters and find out everything he could about this creature.

"Alright, let's get you in some water. First, let me cut that off of you." He reached in with the scissors and cut the rubber band off the first claw. She immediately opened it as if to say *back off*. He would, but first the other. He freed the other claw, the power claw. She snapped it open and closed a few times showing her power.

"That wasn't so bad now was it?" *I'm talking to a lobster. Damn right.* And he saved her life tonight. Danny reached up to put the scissors on the table.

Never take your eyes off a lobster. He just learned this the hard way. The claw was like a vise on his helpless finger. The pain was instant like catching your finger in the car door. He shrieked and stood up fast. She didn't let go, as she dangled in the air. He screamed again. Her power claw was locked on his pinky. She had the upper hand – literally. He shook his hand, begged, "Please!"

The wall was there and the pain almost made him smash her up against it. He didn't, though. He did the dance of pain right there in the middle of his kitchen. His eyes found the tank and he lowered her into it. She let go and seemed to take a deep breath once in the water.

"Fuck! Shit!" He shook his hand and the pain slowly went away. Now he laughed. He laughed hard. He laughed at himself. He laughed at all the people in the restaurant. He pictured his neighbor looking out his window at him dancing around the kitchen with a lobster hanging from his pinky. He laughed.

Danny caught his breath. Looking down at his hand he saw no signs of blood. He pulled up a chair, turned it around backward and sat down in front of the tank.

"What a night, huh? You know, if you only knew how close you were to being boiled you wouldn't have done that." Something dug into his leg. He put his hand in his pocket and pulled out the ring and stared at it for a long moment. "She said no. I guess that was a good thing for you."

For several more minutes Danny Bolick sat in his kitchen and talked to a lobster. His lobster. A lobster he saved from a torturous death. He wished somebody had saved him.

Chapter 7

It had been two days since she said no. Danny still wore the clothes he had on that night. He hadn't shaved, hadn't bathed, and hadn't answered his phone that now had the number twelve by the message box.

He spent a lot of time in the bathroom, not really doing anything just trying to grasp what to do with himself. This is not where he thought he would be on this day.

He stared at the mirror and rubbed his hand on his unshaven face. This is the longest he had gone without shaving in awhile and the grays were there. Man, were they there, mostly on his chin. What was next?

He had put the tank in the tub in case they both needed to hide at a moment's notice.

The lobster kept him company. He would lean in close to look at her. She was miserable too. They needed a life.

A knock at the door made him freeze. He and the lobster lay as still as a couple of lobsters in a tank. He got a visual of lobsters crammed in a tank and couldn't shake it. The knock was there again.

"Yo Danny! You in there?" It was Brad. He rarely went two days without seeing Brad as well. The screen door closed and he heard the net by the pool being picked up off the concrete.

He should go out there and talk to him. What would he say? Brad looked up to him. He didn't want to be a loser in Brad's eyes. He started to get up but sat back down. Maybe later.

He closed his eyes and saw the tank full of lobsters. It hit him like a vision. He knew what he needed to do. Danny looked into the tank, smiled and said, "You need a mate, or a friend in there with you, a companion. The grocery store on 3rd Street has live lobsters. That's what we'll do today."

He stood up and picked the tank out of the tub and placed it on the floor. "I need some water too." The weirdness of talking to a lobster left a day ago. He didn't even think about it now.

He turned on the hot water and then the cold. Steam started filling the room. He stepped in and closed the shower curtain. He turned around and let the hot water beat on his shoulders. This was the best he felt in two days. He now had something to do, something to take his mind off of her. A plan. He washed shampoo out of his hair. He had direction. His lobster needed a companion.

After twenty minutes the water had pickled him and his hands enough. He turned off the water, grabbed a towel and dried off. He used the towel to wipe off the mirror so he could shave. The tank on the lobster's glass had fogged as well. He put on some shaving cream and knelt down to the tank, "You alright in there?" Then he saw *her* name, still written on the back of the lobster's shell, "You need a bath as well my friend." he opened the door below the sink and pulled out a scrub brush. He reached in the tank avoided the now open claws and picked her up behind her head. Wrapped in a towel and with shaving cream still on his face Danny gave his lobster a bath. He scrubbed, but her name managed to stay. He gave up.

He stood up and put his straight razor under some hot water and then shaved the gray off his face.

After shaving and putting on deodorant, he felt like a new man. The tank was slippery from the steam but he managed to pick it up and return it to the claw-foot tub. "You'll be alright in here until I find a more permanent spot for you."

Now, where the hell are the car keys? He hadn't needed them or thought of them for days. They weren't on the kitchen table, or the counter. Maybe he left them in the door. Cautiously, he looked out the door. Brad was not there. He opened it and looked at the keyhole. Nothing there. He shut the door.

He was getting frustrated. Little things had quickly pissed him off the last few days and this was about to make him boil over. *I just need my keys.* He went back in the bedroom. *They have to be here somewhere.* He picked up the khakis he had been wearing that night from the hamper and heard that wondrous jingle.

After a deep breath he peered into the bathroom and said, "I'll be right back." He walked to the door with a little pep in his step until he looked into the driveway. *The truck!* It was a few blocks away. He had parked down the street to make it look like he wasn't home. He decided that was a good thing and some fresh air would do him good. He walked back through the house.

As he passed the bathroom he shouted, "I got everything under control." He unlocked the front door and realized he had never left house this way. He always used the back door. *New things*, he thought. *A new day.*

Danny looked around before climbing into his truck. He still couldn't shake that feeling of eyes on him. As he climbed in he wiped the sweat off his brow. The end of summer was still ending. The two-block walk had brought on the sweat. He was worn out as well. Was he getting old and out of shape like most everyone else his age? After googling 'lobsters,' he was going to google gyms. He started the engine on the second crank and drove off to the Piggly Wiggly.

Outside of the Piggly Wiggly he grabbed a grocery cart. While he was here he might as well get some food. Food he thought. What do lobsters eat? He needed to feed her too. Maybe some shrimp or a small fish.

On aisle four he passed by the cereals and then stopped. *I haven't bought cereal in years. I wonder if they still make Sugar Smacks.* He almost went for the Captain Crunch, but remembered for some reason it always tore up the roof of his mouth. *Cheerios were healthy, right?* He tried remembering that commercial. *Something about the heart? Yikes, I'm debating cereal.* He decided on the Honey Nut Cheerios and then moved along. As he pushed along, he realized one thing. There were people all around him and none of them were staring at him. Progress he thought. Baby steps. The end of the aisle brought him back down. Pancakes.

He stopped and stared at them. Countless times. He thought of the mornings she would sit at the kitchen table checking her Facebook page while he made her pancakes. She was so beautiful in the mornings, wearing pajama bottoms and one of his t-shirts. They were so comfortable together. Where did he go wrong? She seemed to be happy. She seemed to love him. She— she said no. He tried to make excuses for her. Maybe she was just nervous in front of others. Maybe he should call her. She may have changed her mind. He was sick without her. Just hearing her voice would do him good. He thought of that old country song "Achy Breaky Heart." Boy, did he have one. And it was physical pain. His chest hurt. He leaned all his weight on the grocery cart and tried to come to terms with one obvious thing. He had been dumped. He looked around him. No one was watching. This was not the place to dwell on her. He moved on.

The row with the frozen foods was freezing. He shivered and got goose bumps. The back of his shirt was still damp from sweat and now cold against his body. Maybe that's why he bypassed the ice cream and frozen cakes, but right now they were not appetizing. He would hurry through this row, live in the present, no frozen food.

The seafood section was in the back of the store. Being a coastal grocery store, this section was huge. There it was right in the middle of it all. A giant tank stacked three deep with lobsters. He shivered again and looked away. It looked just like the one in the restaurant. He avoided it and decided to get the shrimp first. This part of the store had its own smell. He used to love it, but now he just smelled death. Carcasses everywhere, lying on ice. Stolen from the sea. He felt his gag reflex; he needed to get out of here. *I'm losing it* he thought. First, he would get what he came for.

He pushed his cart faster than normal straight for the lobster tank. He leaned in and gazed at these magnificent creatures. He felt their misery. Their claws were all bound. And they just lay on top of each other with no room to spread out. The smaller were ones on the bottom. Soon they would be boiled, put out of their misery.

That one, he thought. He would get one off the bottom that seemed to be crushed against the glass by the others. He looked around. Where's the help? Is he supposed to reach in there himself? He looked around the tank for something to pick them up with. There were cute drawings of lobsters all around. All so happy to see you, with their boiled red faces. It was sad. *This is cruel. Does no one else feel this way?* Nope, no way would he ever eat this creature from the—

"Can I help you?" said a voice right behind him, jolting him up.

"Yes. Uh. I'm the one with . . . I need a lobster."

"Okay." The high school boy with his summer job looked at him a little weird. He reached underneath the tank and grabbed a pole with pincers at the end. "Did you have a particular one in mind?"

Giddy, like a child in a pet store he turned back to the tank. He now wanted them all. A thought came to him about doing something about this cruelty. No one seemed to care. No one did anything. He cared, but what could he do? He couldn't afford to buy them all. Lobsters weren't cheap. But, the—

"I can come back if you like," the irritated pimpled boy said.

"No no. I'll take that one," he pointed again to the one on the bottom.

"Figures," he could have sworn he heard him say. Danny was getting a little angry at the whole situation. The punk kid with attitude. These people, just walking by the tank as if nothing was wrong, or even worse, peering into the tank as if it were some kind of show.

As the kid climbed a small stool and reached the pole in the tank to retrieve his lobster, Danny realized this *was* all for show. The tank was on display, in the middle for all to see. Come see them before you eat them.

"The box. I said can you *please* hand me that box!" Irritation filled the boy's voice at having to repeat himself.

For a quick moment Danny thought about adding this kid to the display, but thought better of it. He grabbed a box and handed it to him.

The boy with the put the lobster in the box and closed the lid, "Will there be anything else?"

Danny didn't reply and so Justin just walked away. There would be something else. He put the box in his cart and headed for the check out. He looked back at the display. Glass held them trapped. Helpless. One thing he knew for sure, he would return – for more lobsters.

CHAPTER 8

DANNY DEBATED WHETHER to hide the truck again or pull into his driveway. He wished he had a full garage with a door, but he didn't. He decided he couldn't hide forever and pulled into his driveway, into the garage with his back end sticking out. He grabbed his groceries in one arm and with the other carefully picked up the box with his second lobster.

As he walked to the back door he looked over to his neighbor's house. No one seemed to be around.

He entered the house with conviction. He couldn't wait to get his two new friends together. Two grocery bags were set on the counter and with perishables left out. The box was carefully laid on the table. He opened the top to get a peek. His new buddy wasn't as big as the other and the freckles were less prominent, but he was a sight to see nonetheless. Danny noticed one of his antennas had broken off, and his large claw had a significant gash in it. "You're safe now, friend." Danny smiled and decided, since he was no longer hiding, he would put the tank out in the open as well. He headed for the bathroom.

The tank was fairly heavy and sloshed back and forth as he returned and put it on the kitchen table. A little water spilled out. It needed more water, anyway, and he would grab some more from the ocean later. For now, he wanted them to meet. Danny smacked his hands together and rubbed them back and forth. "Look what I brought you," he said with eagerness and pulled out the lobster from the box. Its legs flailed and bound claws moved back and forth.

"Ah, yes. No need for those." He put the lobster in his left hand and walked over to the drawer and pulled out some scissors. He unclipped and freed the claws. They immediately went for him, but he had learned that lesson and kept his fingers behind the lobster.

Back at the tank, he lowered the flailing lobster down into the water. What happened next, he never even thought of. The two lobsters now showed their freed claws and took up defensive positions. Like two mighty scorpions they prepared to battle. The water swayed with tension. Danny looked around in confusion. Would they attack each other leaving him with two dead lobsters? Just then the back door opened.

Brad shouted, "Where the hell have you been? I figured you and the missus eloped." He noticed the tank and the two angry lobsters and one confused Danny.

"Shit," Danny shouted. "They hate each other. I have to get one out. Get me ahh . . shit!"

"Move over Sally," without regard Brad thrust his hand into the stirring water and picked the new lobster up behind the head right where the claws could not get to him. The flapping legs threw water at them like a dog getting out of the pool. "Where do you want him?" he asked Danny. "Is this our dinner?"

"No! Uhh, over here." Danny pulled some dishes out of the sink.

Brad laid the lobster down who froze with claws open ready to strike. "Pretty cool boss man. Where did you get them?"

Danny smiled and exhaled, "Long story."

"Where's *Mrs.* Bolick?" Brad asked in a mocking voice. The blank look on Danny's face told him all he needed to know, and he shook his head.

"Ahh, dude I'm sorry," he looked around for something else to talk about. "You wanna put some of that water from the tank in the sink?"

After a pause, Danny said, "Yeah, that's a good idea, but we need something more permanent." He looked around, then out the window toward the pool. He stared at it for a long moment.

"We have to drain the pool."

"What!" shouted Brad, "Are you for real?"

"Absolutely, I'll explain later. Can you do me a favor?"

"Alright," Brad said, "You okay, Danny?"

Danny gave a hollow, "Yes." His mind was elsewhere. He returned to the tank and peered in.

Brad looked at him and could tell something bad had happened. He had no idea what to say so he said nothing. He turned and looked at a now more relaxed lobster in the sink.

Danny rose and stated, "We have to drain the pool. Can you do that for me?"

Not really understanding the situation, Brad just replied, "Sure, man. I'll do it right now," he exited out the back.

"Thanks, man." Danny returned to the kitchen table and sat down looking at his lobster. Debating his next move.

It took five hours for the pool to drain, and Brad returned around six. Danny was in the now empty concrete shell of the pool, washing the chlorine off the walls with the hose.

Brad sat down and put his legs over the edge. After a long silence he said, "I take it the lobsters are going in the pool?"

"Yep."

"We're gonna need a lot of seawater," Danny turned to him and smiled. That was the cool thing about Brad, he thought. He was on board and didn't need an explanation as to *why* there where lobsters in the house, and where Stacy was.

Danny looked up to him and blocked the glaring sun with his hand, "I figured we'd get as many large trash cans as will fit in *The Cubicle* and take her out, fill 'em up and return. You think you can help with that?"

"No problem man."

"It'll probably take a few trips."

"Are we gonna fill the entire pool?"

"Nah, I figure just the deep end. It should hold about fifty lobsters with plenty of room to keep them from fighting."

"We're . . . getting *more* lobsters?"

"Yep," Danny said and he looked back to the deep end.

"Where are we going to get them from?" Brad tried to get an understanding of what was going on.

"Grocery stores. Restaurants. Probably from the tanks where they are stored at the pier."

"Are you gonna . . . *buy* them?"

Danny paused and then looked back to him, "Nah, they were stolen from the sea . . . I'm going to steal them back." He said this as one would say they were going out and would be back in a few minutes.

Brad poked a little more, "Are you like a lobster savior now?"

Danny laughed, "Something like that. Can you keep this a secret?"

Brad didn't even pause, "Sure. I was getting tired of cleaning out those damn leaves anyway." They shared a laugh.

Brad stared at him for a moment, and figured now was a good time for him to ask. "About Miss Stacy?"

"She said no!" Danny didn't mean for it to sound rude, but it echoed off the empty pool walls.

Brad didn't ask any more questions. Danny would talk about it when he wanted to. He stood up, "I'm gonna go 'borrow' some trash cans."

"I don't want to get you in trouble," Danny said.

"Come on. I'll put them back when we're done. Besides they can't live in your kitchen sink can they?" Brad could sense this new bond Danny somehow had obtained with lobsters of all things was connected to Stacy.

"Alright," Danny said after pondering this. "But I'll get the lobsters myself."

"You're the boss."

"I'll meet you back here in twenty minutes. I've got two trashcans. Can you get your two?"

"Yeah," Brad looked around, "I figure we can fit about twelve in the boat. Leave the rest to me."

"Alright." His neighbor was a friend, "And Brad . . . thanks."

"No worries." Brad turned and walked away. He knew something was off here. His friend had been dumped, and if it took putting a few lobsters in the pool to make him feel better, well . . . he was going to do his part to help. He thought to himself, *Fifty lobsters?*

CHAPTER 9

THE SWEATSHIRT HAD been a good idea earlier, since they were out in open water, but after forty minutes of scooping water into the garbage pails, Danny decided to take his off. Brad hadn't even worn one for the trip. He was young and still proving that he was a man.

They hadn't spoken much since leaving the dock. Brad was giving him his space. They could have gotten water at the pier, instead of taking the boat out of dry dock, but Danny wanted to go for a ride. Brad decided not to mention the hours they spent preparing the boat for dry dock. Now was not the time to pick on Danny. Danny needed some fresh air, and Brad always jumped at the chance to take out *The Cubicle*, especially nowadays, because Danny let him skipper the boat, and even more recently had let Brad dock the boat. That was something his father would never have allowed. Brad was happy to help.

"Let's take a break," Danny shouted from the starboard side. Brad was all too happy to oblige. This was hard work. They had filled three-fourths of the garbage cans. Brad figured they had a couple hundred gallons.

He heard a beer pop open, and then another. In the three years he had known Danny he had never offered him a beer. Tonight was different. They were two men, out on the ocean, working on a cause.

"One beer," Danny said, "and don't tell Kenny." They banged cans together and each took a long drink. Brad took another and they shared half a beer in silence.

Finally, Brad broke the silence, "So, Danny . . . what's going on? Should I be worried about you, bro?"

Danny took a long sip and then let out a belch, to soften the mood. "It was pretty bad, man," he stated. "There were probably thirty people around watching, including the entire kitchen staff." He took another drink, "There I was, on one knee mind you, the maître d' cut the diamond free from the claw. It was about to be a perfect proposal and then she gave me the 'we have to talk' line."

Brad looked at him and gave him the 'that's harsh' face, but said nothing.

Danny continued, "It's weird. I don't remember much of what happened next. I mostly remember eyes. Everyone's eyes . . . on *me.*" He looked out into the ocean, "I just ran, man. I bolted past her, past the maître d', kitchen staff, and all the onlookers." He turned back to Brad, "For some reason I exited through the kitchen. I was almost at the back door when I saw her. The lobster. She was right next to the boiling water. I felt responsible for her, I guess. So I took her. There was to be no engagement, so then, there was to be no boiling of my lobster. Kinda silly, I guess."

"Nah man," Brad added, letting him know he was among friends. "That's pretty cool, actually. You turned something negative into something positive."

Danny looked to him and thought about it for a moment, then agreed, "Yeah, that's it."

"So why all this seawater?" he asked.

"I don't really know. I was at the grocery store because I figured she would need a companion, right?"

"Naturally," Brad added as if it were what anyone would do.

"They were just stacked one on top of the other. I just . . . I just felt something calling me. I thought, this is wrong; I have to do something about this. People were walking around them like it was no big deal. I can't allow it. I won't allow it."

They both thought about it for a moment and then Brad spoke, "Well, some people save whales. You save lobsters."

"That's right," replied Danny. And they both had a big laugh. Danny was glad Brad was there. He understood. He doubted anyone else would.

They threw their empty beers back in the cooler and returned to work, joking and talking now that they were on the same page, "You're gonna need a nickname."

"A nickname?" Danny asked.

"Yeah, so far I've got either *The Lobster Bandit* or *The Shellfish Saint*."

"Hmmm. I like them both," Danny smiled. This was the best he had felt since the incident.

Brad added, "And I'm thinking a costume."

"Don't push it."

"I'm serious."

"We'll see," he smiled, but wondered to himself, was he letting Brad too close to this? He was going to start stealing lobsters, and that was illegal, even if he were the . . . Shellfish Saint.

They returned around nine. Danny backed the boat into the driveway, something he had yet to allow Brad to do. He was able to get right up to the edge of the pool. Brad was impressed that it only took Danny two tries.

Danny put the car in park and joined Brad at the rear of the boat. Brad put out his hand and helped Danny up. Together they emptied twelve fifty-gallon trashcans into the pool. The water gathered at the deep end and created a small pool.

"Not bad," Danny said. "One more trip?"

"Yeah, let me just tell Mom I'm gonna be late. I'll meet you back here in five." He jumped down and ran home. Danny sat on the edge of the boat and looked into the pool.

Car lights broke the darkness as they entered the driveway. It was Kenny. He had called about ten times only to get the answering machine. He parked beside the truck in the grass and got out.

"What's going on?" Kenny asked, looking at how close the boat was to the edge of the pool.

"Nothing," Danny lied as he jumped down from the boat. "Sorry, I haven't picked up."

"You alright, man?" Kenny put his hand on Danny's shoulder.

Danny pulled away. He was feeling a little better now that he had his mind on something else, but he wasn't quite ready to explain it to Kenny. Kenny would surely report back to Stephanie who surely had Stacy's ear.

"You can report to Stephanie that I'm doing fine and that I'll survive," not sure where that came from, but he practically yelled at Kenny.

"Come on man, it's me." Kenny followed him, "Can I do anything?"

"You can give me my space!" There it was again. Why was he taking it out on him? He *was* sleeping with the enemy, but Kenny was his oldest friend. He tried to say something again, this time putting his hand on Kenny's shoulder, "I'm sorry, man. I'm a little fucked up right now. Okay?"

Brad came running up, "You ready?"

"Ready for what?" asked Kenny.

Brad just turned and got in the passenger seat.

"Nothing," Danny said. "Just give me a couple more days. I swear, I'll explain everything." He felt bad, but turned and joined Brad in the truck. He cranked it twice and leaned out the window, "I'll call you this weekend."

"You better," he heard Kenny say as he looked in the rear view. Kenny got back into his car – worried.

CHAPTER 10

IT WAS TWO in the morning by the time Danny got into bed. He and Brad had made three more trips and filled up a good portion of the deep end with ocean water. It was dark and you had trouble seeing the bottom.

He had put the second lobster in the pool. It felt good to see him able to scurry around, mainly *away*. Danny waded in the shallow water for a few minutes and enjoyed the quiet of late night before returning indoors.

He kept his first lobster in the tank by the bed. He refreshed her water, "I swear in a day or two I'll put you in the pool as well." He had at least changed her water.

He clicked the light off. He was exhausted. His arms were killing him. He would be sore tomorrow. It would be a good night's sleep. He started thinking about the *Piggly Wiggly* and that it was open 24/7. The *heist* would have to be done at night – late at night. He turned in the bed, trying to go to sleep. He couldn't quiet his thoughts. *It had to be done in the middle of the night.* After a deep breath, he turned on the light. Danny looked into the tank, "Why not tonight?"

Fifteen minutes later, he was in his truck headed to the *Piggly Wiggly*. After a few minutes of planning, he had gone into the back of the closet and retrieved last year's Halloween costume. The costume had been a failure. No one got that he was the Sleeping Prince from *Spaceballs* at the party; everyone thought he was passed out when he was only playing the part. The wig on the other hand was great. Along with the mustache, many people there said they hardly recognized him. It looked real enough and the best thing about it was it was blond. If they had cameras, the suspect would have blond hair, not brunette like himself.

He decided he would scope it out first. If too many people were around or it didn't seem easy enough he would come up with a better plan, another day. What *that* would be he didn't know. There was no plan B and frankly, there was no plan A. He parked around the corner. Looking in the rear view he adjusted his wig. He had trimmed the mustache so it didn't look as ridiculous. He also added the bottom half of the goatee, which he didn't wear at the Halloween party. He took a deep breath and pulled a baseball cap down low on his head.

"We'll just scope it out," he said to the lobster in the tank that was strapped in with the seat belt on the passenger side. "If I'm not back in ten minutes, you'll need your own plan B." he opened the door and walked toward the front doors.

He counted only four cars in the parking lot. *That's not bad*, he thought. So he grabbed a grocery cart from outside and "the Sleeping Prince" or rather the Shellfish Saint entered the *Piggly Wiggly*.

The grocery cart's left front wheel made more noise than he wanted, but he also wanted to blend in as a shopper. The electric doors roared open. The check-out clerk gave him the quickest of glances before returning to his smart phone. *There is no way he would remember any description with that quick of a look.* So far so good, he looked around for cameras but mainly kept his head low. He proceeded down aisle five to the back of the store.

In the very back, he could hear someone behind the frozen fish doing something. A machine sound seemed to be cutting something. A swinging door separated them. There didn't appear to be anyone else around. He rolled up to the tank.

His heart started pounding now. He suddenly knew he was going to do this . . . and now. He was going to break the law. Without hesitation, he grabbed the pole from under the tank and started boxing lobsters and stacking them in the cart, all the time looking around for any eyes.

There must have been twenty-five lobsters in the tank. This was taking too long. The machine in the back stopped and a silence took over the place. Danny stood frozen. His heart beat inside him so hard he swore he could hear it. He looked at the swinging door and waited. How would he explain this to his father at the police station? He still didn't know about Stacy.

And then the Sea Gods spoke. The machine started up again. Danny moved faster than he had in years. Forgetting about the boxes, he started stacking lobsters right on top of each other into the cart, their legs flapping and clanging against the metal.

Then he saw a shopper all the way at the other end. He should ditch now, but there were still five more to get. It was all or none he decided. The person hadn't looked up and was deciding on bread. Danny furiously plucked the remaining lobsters. He was making too much noise and spilling too much water, but there was no time to wait. He got the last one out, just as the shopper started making his way toward him. He reached in his pocket and did something for Brad. He pulled out a permanent marker and wrote *the Shellfish Saint was here* on the empty tank. He then disappeared into the aisle.

There was no time to think. How was he going to exit? Would he just make a break for it through the front door? He didn't know and as he approached the front of the store he left the cart, walked up and peered around the cookies. The clerk hadn't moved. He was still engaged on his phone.

Twenty-five lobsters in a grocery cart aren't exactly quiet. Danny looked back to the cart. There was a trail of water coming down the aisle. He was going to make a break for it. If he got caught, he got caught. He walked back to the cart, put his hands on the handle and exhaled. He then started walking, not running, but with a pace. The end of the aisle was coming up fast, once out in the open there was no turning back. The place was well lit. He looked up at the bright-as-hell lights that were giving away his presence. He didn't stop.

Just as he came out in the open he heard a terrible noise. The electric front door roared back to life and in walked another customer. Without pause Danny turned the cart, rounded the corner and headed back down aisle five toward the back of the store. Had the person noticed a cart full of lobsters, or the trail of water? This was getting bad. He thought about ditching the cart and making a break for it. He stopped half way down the aisle. *Do something fast.*

So many things could go wrong now. The person shopping in the back could be in the seafood section by now. The worker in the back could be at the tank wondering where all his lobsters were. Or any second the person that just came in could be walking up his aisle. *Stop thinking just go.*

He started pushing the cart again. There must be a back door. *Would it be looked? Would anyone be back there? We're getting ready to find out.* Danny came out into the opening, and sure enough there was the shopper peering into the frozen fish section. The worker must be helping him because he didn't hear the motor. Danny didn't give him another look, as he pushed his cart full of lobsters through the swinging door on the left side, into the back of the store.

He didn't see a soul in sight or the back door. It had to be here somewhere, and then there it was, all lit up calling to him. He approached with caution. He was so close to making this happen. The cart slowed to a crawl and Danny's focus tightened.

All the rear door loading docks for the trucks were closed. There was only this door, but the sign said Caution Alarm. Danny didn't want to set off any alarms so they wouldn't really know when the lobsters went missing – if he got out at all.

He looked back to one of the pull-down doors for the trucks. It was hooked on the bottom, but there didn't seem to be a lock. He walked up to it. He released the hinge and slowly let the door up. Any minute he would hear a deafening alarm and he would have to make a break for it. But there was no alarm, only the smell of fresh air, of freedom. He retrieved the cart and pushed it to the edge of the loading dock. There was no ramp, but at least he was outside. He pulled the door back down behind him.

Well, I made it this far, but how in the hell am I going to get the cart down? His only option was to go get the truck. His truck would be too low to push the cart in but he figured he wouldn't need to lower it by much. It was nice and dark back here. He jumped down to the pavement and landed louder than he wanted to, and then ran as fast as he could to get the truck.

His adrenaline was pounding inside him. He felt like screaming aloud in excitement. This was the most alive he had felt in a long time.

When he returned with the truck he paused before driving all the way back. Nothing seemed to have changed so he gassed it. Half way there, the truck set off a motion light. The damn thing was as alarming as the sun. He didn't slow down – too close to give up now. He saw the cart up on the fourth loading dock and backed in. He opened the door and looked to his passenger seat, "I got you some more friends."

Danny jumped into the back of his pick-up. It was about a foot and a half too low. Turning the cart sideways to get a good grip, he lifted with all his might and leaned back.

He shouldn't have leaned back.

The weight overwhelmed him, and for all to hear, Danny turned and let the grocery cart fall into the back of truck. Metal smacking metal echoed off the walls. Lobsters went in all directions inside the bed of the truck.

He was sure someone would be coming out the back door, setting off the alarm. He jumped down and ran around the truck checking to see that no lobsters had fallen out. Sure enough there was one, limping away in the dark. Danny grabbed him and jumped back in the truck.

Knowing not to put him in the tank with his original lobster, he set him on the floor on the passenger side. No one came out the back door and no more lights came on. Danny put the car in drive and the Shellfish Saint drove away with his catch.

CHAPTER 11

THE NEXT MORNING, Danny awoke to a horrifying sound. He thought he might be dreaming so his tried to stay in a dream state, but it was there again – a forceful knock at the back door. The kind of knock a cop would make. He froze. *They got me. There must have been cameras.* He hid under the covers. *How long do they put you in jail for stealing lobsters?* There it was again. Relentless pounding. They wanted in.

He decided he might as well not go to jail in his pajamas, so he quietly slid out of bed and put on his jeans. He heard voices or a voice. He threw on a t-shirt and went to give himself up.

As he approached the back door he saw blond hair peering through the window, not the kind of hair cops have.

"Danny, wake up! Let me in!" It was Brad. Danny exhaled like he had never done before. *It was only Brad.* He unlocked the door and the sunlight broke in. It was later than he thought.

"Dude!" Brad said excitedly. "There's a bunch of lobsters in the pool! I couldn't count them all!" He followed Danny into the house.

"I know," said Danny, he opened the fridge. "Here," he reached in and pulled out a box of fresh shrimp. He tossed the box across the kitchen to Brad who caught and in one motion set it on the table.

"Where did you get them? *WHEN* did you get them?"

After taking a big drink out of the milk container he said, "I couldn't sleep last night, so I paid a visit to the *Piggly Wiggly*." He returned the milk to the fridge.

"You stole the *Piggly Wiggly's* lobsters?"

"Yep. *All of them.*"

"Oh man!" Brad was excited, "That is classic! And no one saw you?"

"Not sure really. I thought you were the cops. Do me favor, don't knock like that from now on."

"Wow, you really did it."

"And I left a message on the glass."

"You didn't . . . ?"

"*The Shellfish Saint* was here."

Brad lifted his knees to his chest a few times and punched at the air exuberated, "That sir, is impressive. I wonder if you'll make the news."

Danny hadn't thought of that. Maybe leaving the note was too much. He needed to be smart. If he got caught the joke would be over. Still he felt good about it. Out in his back yard were a bunch of lobsters stretching out their legs in the sun, "We should feed them." He picked the box of shrimp off the table, and headed outside.

"After you, boss," Brad opened the door for him and patted him on the back as he walked by.

Danny turned back to him, "Ahh, grab the scissors out of the kitchen drawer so we can free their claws."

"Will do."

For a moment they just stood above the pool admiring the creatures below, not sure how to proceed.

"Guess I should have taken off the rubber bands before I put them in."

"What's with the grocery cart in the pool?" Brad asked.

Danny laughed. "Uh, that was their getaway vehicle. I didn't know where else to put it, so I just let the whole thing go."

"*Let the lobsters hit the floor! Let the lobsters hit the floor!*" Brad sang out loud. Danny looked at him not getting it. Brad added, "You know the song? Let the Bodies Hit the Floor. . . ." no response from Danny, "You're old dude."

Danny just smiled at him, "I'll get a mask out of the garage." He came back with a mask, dive belt and tank.

They had managed to fill the deep end with about three feet of water. Walking there would be hazardous with all the angry claws around, so he convinced Brad that floating just above would be safer.

Brad donned the gear and then braved the water. They were too fast under water. He wasn't even coming close to grabbing one. After ten minutes he gave up. There needed to be a plan B.

Plan B made use of the grocery cart. Danny put the cart in water keeping the top half from going under the water. Brad used the net to fish them out. One by one he scooped up the lobsters and returned them to the cart. Danny sipped a beer as held the grocery cart in place. They laughed and enjoyed the sun. It's not often that you go fishing for lobsters in a pool.

Once he retrieved them, they both stood knee deep in the water with the grocery cart between them. First, reaching in and grabbing a lobster, making sure your hands were in proper place and then freeing the claws. Each time the claws tried to get them, but nature didn't allow their claws to turn 360 degrees. Once freed, they would sit the lobster in the water, who would then turn and scurry into the deep end backward. It took about thirty minutes to free them all. Danny worried they would fight, but the larger space seemed to keep them away from each other.

They got out of the pool and sat with their feet hanging over the edge of the deep end. Danny opened the box. They began throwing shrimp into the pool. "I wonder how long it's been since they've eaten?" Danny asked. There was plenty of movement below the surface as they fed their new found friends.

"We're gonna need more shrimp," Brad added.

"I'll get some later. I have to run an errand," Danny said.

"Where to?"

"I haven't told my father yet. Not sure how many more disappointments he will take from me."

"Don't be too hard on yourself, bro. It's *her* loss."

Danny hadn't really let it out yet and hadn't allowed himself to think of her. He knew this was something he would have to do alone. So he changed the subject. "Listen, thanks for helping on all this."

"No worries, bro. That's what friends are for."

Danny stood up, "I'll pick up some dinner while I'm out. It's the least I can do for you."

"You're not going to the *Piggly Wiggly* are you?" they both laughed.

"Nah, figured I'd scope out *Food Lion* next." they laughed again and Danny went inside.

CHAPTER 12

ON THE WAY to see his dad, he drove slowly. Last time they talked, when he told him he was going to ask her, was the last time he can remember them not getting into a fight. This will no doubt bring out the gloves.

He parked at the pier and sat for a moment before exiting. He really missed mom now.

Beside the pier was *Fresh Ed's*. They sold fresh catch right from the boats. Danny remembered a fairly large tank for lobsters there. Why rush telling Dad? He decided to take a peek at the tanks.

A bell announced his entrance. This place was small compared to the grocery store. He would have to hit it after hours. The lock on the front door had two dead bolts. Not really his expertise. Back doors were proving to be.

A young college girl was working the register. No doubt a family business. Danny browsed around and then decided to ask a few questions.

"Hello," she greeted him with a smile. She was cute and looked a little out of place selling seafood.

"How's it going? Got any lobsters?"

"Nope, only cattle here."

Danny looked confused. *Did she say . . .*

"That was a joke."

"Oh, sorry," they both laughed. "I'm usually faster than that."

"Well, it happens. You're getting on in years."

Did she just . . .

"Again, kidding. They're in the back. Come on, I'll show ya."

A tour. Guess I'm not that old after all. "Is this a family farm?" he flirted back.

She thought about it for a moment before getting it, "There you go." she gave him a smile. She was cute. Danny noticed a few tattoos peeking out of her white tank top. She had less of a tan than most girls around here at this time of year. She was average size. Danny felt a little guilty when he checked out the rest of her as she walked slightly ahead of him. *Great ass.* And it was the first time Danny ever remembered saying to himself *if I were ten years younger.* He *was* getting old.

"It's back here," she said as they went through the swinging door. He sensed that she knew he was checking her out. He also felt that she didn't care. She had dirty blond hair, shoulder length. Danny could tell the guys liked her. He did.

She led him to the back of the store. He didn't see any cameras. She was cute, but he still needed her lobsters. Second thoughts began to creep in.

"Here you go," she pointed to a large filtration tank. He looked in. The water pump was making a lot of bubbles. There they were stacked like bricks. Entombed. He couldn't judge how many were in there, but appeared to be a lot.

He noticed a back door with a modest dead bolt on it. If he did steal these he would have to add breaking and entering to his crime sheet. Danny looked inside the tank, "Nice flirtation system you got here – FILTRAtion!" he quickly corrected red in the face.

She smiled and let him slide, "So how many do you need?"

"Ahh, not sure."

"Just checking out the merchandise?" Then her face changed, "I'm really sorry," she blushed, "I don't know why I'm flirting with you." She thought about what she just said, "And I don't know why I just said that. I'll . . .just . . ."

"Please," he quickly added, "No worries. Really, you made my day. It's nice for someone your age to notice." *Yikes. Where am I going with this? Mumble. Mumble.* "Got any shrimp?"

The way he said it or just the situation made them both start laughing. "You're not here on vacation are you?" she questioned.

"No, no. Born and raised."

"Me too." The bell on the front door broke their moment. She turned to the front, "I better . . . actually, the shrimp are up front."

"Ahh, okay. I need about five pounds."

"Wow. okay. Have you got a date to this party? Sorry. Kidding."

Whatever it was, maybe it was Stacy, maybe it was his guilt, or maybe he had just lost a step, but he didn't ask her out. *She is way too young. I am way too old.* And for the second time in a week Danny panicked and went for the door, "You know. I gotta run some other errands first, I'll be back." He almost ran over the lady who had just entered.

"Okay then," she said with a puzzled tone in her voice.

The bell shouted at him as he opened the door. "Okay, Thanks," he said, sounding like a true jackass.

Once he got far enough away from the store he walked around in a few circles feeling really stupid. *I didn't even get her name.* He felt like an embarrassment to men everywhere. He was never really a ladies' man, but he was better than that crash-and-burn he just did. Then he thought about the lobsters. Maybe she just worked there. He would feel bad if he were taking money out of her family's pockets. There were two things he needed from *Fresh Ed's* – his lobsters, and her name.

"Cattle," he laughed out loud. The smile drifted away as he approached the bar.

Bells ringing on doors were beginning to get on his nerves. He nodded to Paul the bartender. Andy, his dad's quietest friend, was the first to spot him.

"The man of the hour is here," he stood up and announced. So much for being the quiet guy. Danny had no idea how he was going to play this, so he decided he was just going to wing it.

"Howdy, boys." he said, sitting down not sure why he was overly cheerful.

"Well," Larry asked, "If she was smart she said no!" They laughed and took a big drink.

Danny just held up his left hand – the one with no ring on it. They caught on fast and a silence swept in the room.

"Ah jeeze, I'm sorry Danny," Larry apologized. "I didn't mean to say . . ." He was a loss for words.

"Don't sweat it, Larry," Danny said. "Guess she had other plans for her future."

"Figures, you'd screw that up too," his dad mumbled, as he took a drink. He looked embarrassed.

"Sorry, Dad, am I embarrassing you in front of your friends here!" he raised his voice above everyone else.

"Now, now," Larry tried to keep the peace. "Let's just talk about this."

Danny couldn't believe his father was still so distant from him. He couldn't let it slide. "How about how bad you've been as a father!"

Wayne slammed his beer down, "Don't you go blaming me."

Paul the bartender who hears everything was there with a bottle and some shot glasses. He quickly got between them. "Couldn't help but overhear, Danny. I hate that for ya." Paul was a man of few words, but when he spoke he spoke with conviction. He poured out five shots and raised his. "*To bitches and witches who roam the sea. They don't call on you . . .*" This had been recited before in this bar, because Wayne, Larry, and Andy raised their glasses and the four of them finished with, "*They don't call on* me!" they slammed down their shot glasses hard. Paul patted Danny on the back and then returned to the bar.

"She'll be the one to miss *you*," Andy spoke and took a drink of beer. Danny could hear a painful past in his voice as well. He'd been there too.

"They're all the same," Larry added with his beer. Danny felt his news was bringing back bad memories for all of them.

"Hey! Listen to this!" Paul shouted from behind the bar and he turned up the TV.

"How many are gone?" A male reporter asked and stuck the microphone up to a pimply-faced boy.

"All of them," he said. "'Bout fifty I guess."

"You just came in and they were all gone?" the reporter helped move along the story.

"That's right. All they left was this note." Right there on the TV Danny saw his handwriting. He tightened up. Would his dad recognize his handwriting?

"Well, there you have it Jessica. Fifty lobsters just vanished. Apparently taken by the Shellfish Saint. I'm Robert Starnes reporting for *Bay Nine News*."

"Thanks, Robert. Keep us posted on that story."

"Will do," responded Robert. The picture went full to Jessica and the anchor beside her.

"Shellfish Saint?" she stated.

"Bizarre story," he added. "We'll be right back."

Happy to stop talking about lost love, the conversation switched to this terrible theft at the *Piggly Wiggly*.

"Some punk kids probably," Larry said defiantly. "Probably did it on a dare."

George, who always sat at the bar said, "Yeah, well I dare them to come near my boat."

"Here, here," they all added.

"What the hell's a Snailfish Saint, anyway?" asked a bit drunk Andy.

Larry leaned in, "Shellfish Saint, you moron. They stole lobsters not snails."

They all laughed. Andy just took another drink.

Danny needed to get out of there so he just stood up. "Well, I'm gonna head on out."

"Ahh, stay for a beer, Danny boy," Larry said.

"Nah, I got a friend from college in town I got to meet up with." He gave his father a moment to say something. He didn't. Danny turned to leave, "I'll see ya'll later."

"Will do. You keep your head up," Larry added as he looked at Wayne like he was a fool for not talking to his son.

The outside air was cool. The sun was going down and Danny wasn't used to remembering to bring a jacket yet. Even though his dad and his friends were fishermen and made their living off bass and tuna, they had a kinship with all fishermen. Danny hadn't thought of that. If he got caught, he would not be welcome at *The Pier's End* anymore.

He walked up to *Fresh Ed's*. Embarrassed by how he left things with the cute girl at the counter, he decided he would go in and at least get her name. Besides, he needed shrimp. He tried the door, but it was locked. He stepped back and looked around. *They must close at sundown.* He wondered where she hung out at after work. He gave up. *She's too young anyway.*

CHAPTER 13

THE RIDE HOME brought much confusion. What the hell was he doing? He had developed a strange attraction to lobsters and he seemed to be the only one who wanted to help.

He knew it had a lot to do with Stacy. . . . *Stacy*. He thought about driving by her house, or maybe just calling her. Anything. He suddenly needed to hear her voice. His cell buzzed. It was a sign. What if it was Stacy?

He swayed off the road slightly as he reached in his pocket, hoping to see her name. He saw Brad's instead.

"Hey Brad," He knew he couldn't keep the disappointment out of his voice.

"Yo! Where are you?" Brad shouted, "You got the shrimp?"

The shrimp. He forgot the shrimp. "Uhhh, on my way there now. See you in thirty."

Brad laughed, "Don't forget you promised to feed the neighbor as well."

His voice shook, "Ten four. I'll grab some burgers or something."

"You okay?" Brad questioned.

Brad deserved some kind of explanation, but he didn't want to get into it. "Yeah man, just this and that right now. I'll be there in about thirty minutes."

Brad paused, started to say something, and then decided on, "Later."

"Later," he replied, grateful to hang up.

Now where to get the shrimp? It was too soon to go back to the *Piggly Wiggly*. He was going to scope out a small seafood store a few blocks from here. He knew they had tanks. A gravel parking lot popped underneath his tires as he pulled in.

It was a small store that specialized in shellfish. They also carried live bait for the fishing shop next door that sold poles and every other water hunting need. His senses came alive as he walked in the door. No cameras.

The door was one of the few he had entered today that had no bell. He surveyed the room. The lobster tank was right up front on a makeshift table. It was the showpiece of this modest dungeon. A badly drawn lobster sign told of its contents, and of course, colored in with a red marker. It was made of fiberglass and not much bigger than a home fish tank.

"Be there in a minute," a voice said from the back.

The Saint appeared above the waterline and looked in. His heart picked up the rhythm of their situation and made him angry. There were probably only eight, but they needed saving. He looked to the back – still no one.

Without thinking he reached in and grabbed one. He pulled it up and looked into its eyes. Without thinking, he reached for another, and then another, and stacked them under his arms like gathering wood for a fire. He was parked right out front.

"Be right there," he heard again from the back, yet no one came out.

It was too tempting. Six was all he could get. Their sharp legs were digging into his skin. He quietly opened the door and exited without anyone ever seeing him. He ran to the truck and gently laid them in the back. He knew two more were inside. He couldn't leave. *You're gonna get caught,* he thought, but the ease of this was too tempting. He reached in the glove box and retrieved the wig and hat. He ran back inside for the rest quietly opening the door and looking around – still no one. He went for the tank, but just as he was about to reach in—

"Sorry about that." An older portly man came in wiping his hands on a towel and then onto his overalls, "Damn filtration systems gonna drive me to drink," he gave a chuckle. "What can I do for ya?"

A frozen Danny slowly came to, "Uhh, need about three pounds of shrimp."

The man came right up to the lobster tank. *Don't look in, don't look in.* Danny suddenly felt disgusted with himself. He should have been smarter. To get busted like this was dumb. He thought of Brad waiting for him, and he had just come from talking with his dad. However, the man carried on to a large cooler at the side of the store.

"Heading out tonight?"

Danny shivered, "What? Uh, yeah. Gonna do a little fishing."

"Well it's a good night for it." He opened the cooler, scooped out some shrimp and put them on the scale. Danny adjusted his wig. He looked down at his shirt. It was soaked and his arms had scratches on them. *Please let me get out of here. Please.*

The man wrapped the shrimp in a bag and walked behind the counter.

"That be it for ya?"

"Uh yeah," Danny mumbled and tried not to make much eye contact.

The owner pointed to the bill, "That'll be fifteen even."

Danny gave him the money and it seemed to take forever to get the change. He put it right in his pocket. "Thank you." he walked out the door. He noticed water on the floor that he had spilled. That was close.

"'Scuse me?" he heard just as he reached the door. Danny turned and almost put his hands up in defeat.

"You want your shrimp?" The man held out the bag of shrimp.

Danny laughed, "Sorry. Not all there today." Still avoiding eye contact he went back to the register, retrieved the bag, and tried once again to escape. He walked toward the truck and waited for the man to come out with his shotgun. He didn't. So, Danny cranked it twice and drove home.

CHAPTER 14

DANNY PULLED INTO his driveway shortly after seven. It was already getting dark. Summer was leaving and so was the long daylight.

Brad was by the pool with the lobsters. He gave him the WTF look that Brad told him meant "what the fuck" to his generation.

Danny didn't say a word. He got out of the truck and threw the shrimp bag to Brad. He then proceeded to the back of the truck and Brad watched him knowing something was up.

Without speaking, he picked up a lobster in each hand and walked down the bare pool steps in the shallow end. He took the scissors that they had left on the steps and freed their claws and then he let them go right at the edge.

"*The Shellfish Saint* strikes again!" Brad shouted jumping up and down. He ran to the truck to help out and then counted in his head, "Only seven?" he asked perplexed and disappointed.

Danny knelt in the water and let two more go, "I had to leave some behind."

Brad was about to make a joke, but felt that Danny was really bothered by that, "Where'd you get 'em?"

"*Hooks and Bait*, near the pier." He picked up the shrimp bag that Brad set by the deep end.

"That old shack has lobsters?" Brad wondered.

"Yep. I walked in and the old guy that runs the place was in the back. He shouted that he'd be there in a minute. I looked over and saw the tank he kept them in, and the door was right there, so I thought . . . why not? I couldn't carry them all at one time, so I set the first batch in the back of the cab, looked around . . . and went back in."

Brad gasped. "You went back in?"

Danny nodded repeatedly, "I know. Not sure what I was thinking. Could have ended right there. So, I'm about to reach in the tank again and out walks the old man."

"What did you do?" Brad laughed. He was loving the story.

"He asked what he could do for me . . . so I bought three pounds of shrimp," he tossed the bag to Brad.

Brad howled, "You then bought some shrimp! You got *balls* bro, like metal ones."

Danny became quiet. There was more to the episode that he couldn't explain. "I couldn't help myself. I need to learn how to be a better thief."

Brad slapped him on the back, "Dude, you seem to be doing alright. You're stealing them right in daylight."

Danny pondered this. It's true. He has gotten away each time. Brad opened the bag, and set it beside them. They sat in quiet, breaking pieces of shrimp and throwing them in the pool. Danny thought about Stacy and how she will never swim in this pool again. He felt a physical pain in his chest. Then the lobsters helped relax him.

Brad went home around 9:30. They had eaten by the pool and were growing fonder of being around the lobsters.

Danny wondered if Brad's dad wondered what they were up to. From his window, you couldn't see the bottom of the pool, but you could probably tell it had been drained.

Danny finished the dishes and decided he needed to learn more about these creatures he was risking his life for.

He retreated to the bedroom and started his computer. As he waited for it to boot up he threw on some pjs and put on a fresh t-shirt.

He sat down at the computer and thought *Wikipedia* would have the most info. It reminded him of his youth when his father came home with their first set of encyclopedias. As a boy he'd marveled at how many books were in the collection. He used to love the indentions in the books that took you to another letter of the alphabet.

Most of his friends were married now with children of their own. *Wikipedia* was the learning tool now and he doubted any of his friends brought the encyclopedia home for their kids. In some ways Google was killing some nostalgia. Only the public library was still trying to fight the digital age.

He typed in "lobster" and immediately all the info on lobsters was there. *The library doesn't stand a chance.*

He first admired the picture of a beautiful brown lobster on the right. It was taken when it was still alive. Most pictures you see are after they have been boiled and are bright red. Give a kid a crayon he thought and the lobster would always be red. Then he saw them. His bond with lobsters grew as he saw their massacred bodies dressed up with lemon wedges. The pictures were of lobsters on plates with coleslaw beside them or with some other delicatessen about to be eaten. He wondered if he did a search on cows if there would be picture of a hamburger. Cattle. The girl at the store was still in the back of his head.

He started to read. *Clawed lobsters comprise a family (Nephropidae, sometimes also Homaridae) of large marine crustaceans.* Those were some big words he thought. He laughed to himself and thought about Kenny. Every time he or Kenny heard someone say a big word they would always say, "That's a big word – like gymnasium or mayonnaise," then they would just laugh for a few minutes. It was part of their bond. They'd been saying it for years and it never got old. They laughed at the same things. He made a mental note to visit Kenny at work tomorrow and really talk to him. He continued reading.

Lobsters are economically important as seafood, forming the basis of a global industry that nets more than one billion dollars annually. He just sat back and thought about that last sentence, *a billion dollars of lobsters eaten annually. Lobsters are in worse shape than the library.*

He skimmed the rest of the page. Lobsters live in every ocean; they live on rocky, sandy, or muddy bottoms from the shoreline to beyond the edge of the continental shelf.

More big words started to make his attention drift. The girl with jokes at the seafood counter popped back in his head. Had she been flirting with him? She was cute. He wasn't that old. He pictured meeting her father and quickly decided that was a dead end. Besides, he needed her lobsters.

He tried to read some more. He was looking for something. Something to make him say *yes; I'm doing the right thing.*

About halfway down was a whole section with the title Capacity for Pain. He wondered if other animals on *Wikipedia* had this section. The great thing about the Internet is that it's all just one typed word away. He quickly searched cow and saw no section about pain.

It has to be that there were some people who agree boiling a live creature is a terrible thing to do. He went back to the Capacity for Pain section and sure enough there had been studies.

A 2007 study at Queen's University, Belfast, suggested that crustaceans do feel pain. In the experiment, when prawn antennae were rubbed with sodium hydroxide or acetic acid, the animals showed increased grooming of the afflicted area and rubbed it more against the side of the tank.

That's all he needed to see. It was simple to him. Any bound lobster that sat weeks in a tank was only waiting for the most unimaginable death he could think of.

The last text he read gave him shivers. It read: *A common misconception is that a lobster screams when boiled; actually, the whistling sound is steam escaping the shell.*

The whistling sound is steam escaping the shell. He shook the goose bumps off and put his computer to sleep. He looked into his tank at his lobster. "Not on my watch," he said, "and tomorrow I'm gonna let you stretch out with the others, you must be miserable in there."

He quickly climbed in bed and turned out the light. He shuddered. *The whistling sound is steam escaping the shell.*

CHAPTER 15

THE NEXT MORNING, thick clouds rolled over and kept the morning cool. Danny sat by the pool drinking his coffee. The tank was beside him. He stared at his lobster that started it all.

"Well, it's time you join the others. Not fair to keep you in a tank." Danny knew that this scene might seem humorous to someone else but he had grown attached to this lobster. Relaxing by the pool with her seemed like a normal thing to do. He pulled her out of the tank and dried the back of her shell off with a towel. Stacy's name was still there. He decided to leave it and use it as a way of finding her.

After a pause, he got up and walked to the pool. Danny wasn't a religious man, but as he bent down to put his lobster in the water, it felt ritualistic to him, a cleansing of the spirit. And a second chance for a lobster that had been about to be boiled. He remembered something else he had read about lobsters. If not caught for their meat, living to one hundred was not uncommon. A hundred years at the bottom of the sea. *Some of you shall see that day.* He then realized that this pool was not big enough for them and he would have to eventually set them free, but today was not that day.

On his way to see Kenny, Danny kept the window down in his truck. He was feeling new, refreshed. It was time to tell his best friend his little secret.

He pulled into a large parking lot and parked into one of the reserved parking spaces just as he had when he was young. Why break with tradition? Kenny used to buck the system too with him, but now one of the spaces had his name on it.

The outside building was square just like the boxes they sold. In one way, Kenny had it made. Joining his father's business had afforded him a house on the water and a BMW in his parking spot by the front door. But in another way, Kenny was cursed. Who wouldn't say yes to that paycheck? The downside was that selling boxes had zero excitement. The days blurred.

Danny once made Kenny a round box. It took him a couple of hours to make it. He strolled into the square building throwing it up in the air. He threw it at Kenny. He didn't get the joke. Age can change a man. At work, Kenny was a different man, and one with a secretary.

"Hi Margaret," Danny said to the longest running employee at *Cardboard Containers*. He never knew why she didn't like him, but Marge always gave him the cold shoulder.

"He's busy," a voice answered. She didn't look up.

"Great, thanks," he said as he continued inside. Kenny was on the phone, so he browsed the walls. Over the years, the office decor had changed. Now there were fewer photos of the good old days and more cheap paintings with no heart. Danny made one a little crooked just to see if he could get a rise out of Kenny. Kenny smiled and rolled his eyes.

"Well, get me the total today, please," Kenny said to the phone and then hung up. "You seem to be feeling better."

Danny sat down in the chair across from his desk and threw his feet up on it, "Oh, you know, Marge always knows how to cheer a guy up."

They laughed and Kenny got up and shut the door. "I'm glad you came by. I'm worried about you."

"Don't be. I'm doing alright. Pretty good actually, all things considered," a slight crack in his voice hinted there was more.

"You haven't returned any of my calls." Kenny sat back down behind his desk.

Danny paused for a moment. He had not been a good friend lately. "I know. My bad. Kinda put it past me I guess and don't want to talk about it."

"You can't keep it balled up inside you. It's not healthy." Kenny looked to Danny with a sincere look of concern. This bothered Danny. It gave him guilt.

"I'm okay, seriously. I'm a new person, actually. I have found something that has changed my perspective on things."

Kenny leaned forward, interested, "You met someone already?"

"I didn't say *someone*. I said *something.*" He looked around. How was he going to explain this?

"Good for you. But why do I suddenly feel like I don't want to hear this?" Kenny said, confused, as he leaned back in his chair.

Danny was having second thoughts about telling him, or at least telling *work* Kenny, "How about I tell you over a beer?"

Kenny paused and studied him, "No. Tell me now."

Danny stood up. He made up his mind that this was not the place to tell him. The work Kenny was different. He didn't need a lecture about it, because he wasn't even sure how he could defend it. "This Friday. Stop by for some beers after work. And don't bring Stephanie; tell her it's a guy thing."

Kenny's interest level climbed higher, "Now I'm really worried. What's going on with you?" he was sitting up in the chair again.

Danny shrugged and started for the door; anything to get away, "Nothing."

Kenny balled up a piece of paper and threw it at him, "Tell me." His phone rang. Thank the heavens his phone rang. "This is Kenny," he gave Danny the hold-on finger.

Danny gave him the middle finger and mouthed *Friday.* He left and shut the door behind him. Margaret didn't look up from her computer as he walked by.

Danny spoke to her head, "Marge, always a pleasure." He walked out of the square box.

That was weird. Danny was not fitting into this grown-up world. Kenny had grown up and did the standard "get married and have a baby" thing. Kenny even had a picture of *his* wife and *his* baby on *his* desk in *his* office. Work for Dad and make him proud. Danny was thirty-eight and had none of that. He had an old truck that took two cranks to start.

There was no baby out there that needed him to survive. No wife waiting at home for his love. No job where people expected him to take care of things.

Danny stopped. He suddenly realized that there was no one who needed him.

Except Lobsters. Lobsters need me. People saved whales or made sure that the turtles had a place to bury their eggs. Birds had sanctuaries and the endangered had friends. Lobsters had Danny, and he now held on to this with a tight grip. He was never more sure of anything in his life. He was in fact *The Shellfish Saint*.

He searched his memory and thought of the *Food Lion* on 8th St. They housed such lobsters. They weren't open 24/7. After eleven there would be no one there.

He would need hardware. Caged lobsters were protected by steel. Inside the *Home Depot* he would find what he needed. He drove there with a newfound energy.

"These will cut through that lock you lost your keys to," said the man in the orange apron as he handed Danny some bolt cutters. The nose dropped to the floor. They were massive and heavy, about two feet long.

Danny smiled. He had his power claw. Now he needed his second claw. "I also need a good pair of wire cutters," he stated.

"No problem, next aisle over. Follow me." People at the *Home Depot* were helpful and friendly.

As he checked out at the counter, he wondered if he looked suspicious. The clerk rang up one bolt cutter, a large pair of wire cutters, two cans of black spray paint, a sledge hammer, one pair of tight fitted leather gloves, a Swiss Army knife, one heavy duty flashlight, and three permanent black markers.

"Your total comes to one fifteen seventy-six," the clerk said with the friendly *Home Depot* smile.

Guess there's nothing suspicious here. I'm just doing yard work. Danny swiped his card.

CHAPTER 16

JUST AROUND MIDNIGHT, Danny pulled in behind the Food Li-on. Gone was the wig and mustache, replaced with black clothes. He pulled his black ski mask over his face and exited the truck. In the back of his truck's cab he grabbed a backpack and threw it over his shoulder. He left the bolt cutters and sledgehammer. They were too heavy. First he would scope the place out.

It was dark with only one light illuminating the back door. Danny kept to the shadows. He had no idea how he would get in. There was no way he could bust down the backdoor. It was too heavy, so he by-passed it.

The large air-conditioning motor was fenced in. Maybe there was a way in on the other side of the ten-foot fence. It was too high to climb, so Danny pulled his left claw, the wire cutters, out of his bag. He slow-ly cut an opening for him to fit through. Using the bag first, he pushed through like a true thief.

The machines were loud. He didn't like the noise and moved quickly to find the door. He pondered going back and getting the sledgeham-mer, but decided to look around first. He walked around some more loud cooling machines. The area here was vast. Then he saw his open-ing. There was a window by an office. He pulled some duct tape out of his bag and hurried toward it.

He looked around, saw no one, and put a large X of tape over the window and then a few other stripes. He wasn't sure where he learned this from but figured it would work. Then he looked around for something heavy. Beside the door was a brick used to prop it open. *Perfect.* He retrieved it and stood in front of the window.

I'm the Shellfish Saint. I'm the Shellfish Saint.

He covered his face and reared back with the brick. He took a deep breath and then struck the tape-covered glass. The engines muffled the collision, but the glass didn't break.

It's got to be more than a love tap, Danny.

Without a breath he reared all the way back with the brick and struck the glass with full force. It was loud. The window collapsed on itself and fell to the ground in large pieces. His ears were ringing. The engines were screaming and there seemed to be another noise that made his eyes widen. He had set off the alarm.

No time to think, just do it. He put the bag on the base of the frame to protect against the charred glass and climbed in, or more like rolled in. He fell to the ground around the broken glass. *Better move fast.* He got up and ran. Having no idea where he was, he figured he'd take the hall that led to the middle. He ran down the hall and saw the swinging door to the main section of the store. There was a grocery cart that he retrieved just before crashing through the door.

A surge of emotion came over him. There they were, on display just like at the *Piggly Wiggly.* He had to be successful or it would be too late for them.

He wondered how much time he had as he filled the grocery cart with flailing lobsters. Glancing around he saw no one, but there was a screaming alarm and it was screaming at him.

His adrenaline was flowing. He grabbed lobsters by the tail, by the claw, by the leg, whatever was there first. *I should have parked down the street. Idiot.* He put his signature on the tank and ran.

He steered about fifteen lobsters to the back of the store the same way he came in. Once in the back, he took a different route and headed for the back door. Down the hall and around the corner the wheels of the grocery cart howled and shook as he ran full bore.

There was a camera facing the back door, but he was prepared for that. He crept up behind it and unzipped his bag. He grabbed a nearby stool and Danny the Thief climbed on it and spray painted the front of the camera. He noticed his hands were shaking, but he was also proud that he thought to buy paint. He jumped from the stool, unlocked the dead bolt, and swung open the door. There was a ramp that led down to parking lot. His truck was waiting to make the final exit.

He grabbed the cart from the front and yanked it forward as his leg held open the door. Once out, he pushed the cart hard from behind and then jumped on it, just as he had done as a kid, and rode it like a chariot all the way down the ramp.

The ramp was too steep and the speed became too much. His eyes showed fear as things took a turn for the worse. He tried to jump down and slow the cart down with his legs but they wouldn't move fast enough. He lost his grip and slid to his stomach. The cart sped ahead of him and crashed into the front of his truck. The back wheels bounced up with the lobsters and then crashed down silent.

The thundering alarm made him jump to his feet fast. He grabbed the cart and wheeled it to the side of his pickup. Again, he picked up lobsters two at a time, by tails or whatever was sticking out. He noticed his forearm was scraped badly from the fall, but he didn't slow down to access the damage. Two cranks later – he was gone.

After a few turns he slowed to a normal speed and tried to catch his breath. He checked the rear view for the cops and their flashing lights. No one appeared. He let out a scream and hit the steering wheel a couple of times in celebration and let the adrenaline out. He headed across town and his heart rate began to slow down. *The Shellfish Saint* had struck again.

Ten minutes later he passed another grocery store and came to a stop at the red light. *I forgot that one was there.* The light turned green. He sat in the truck for a moment and took a deep breath. There were still a few hours of darkness. He smiled. *Why not?* There seemed to be no one around, so Danny did a U-turn and pulled into the shopping mall.

This place was fairly new. It housed many stores all along one strip. He remembered when this was all woods. He drove past the closed *McDonald's* and the *Dollar Store*. Everyone's lights were off for the night. The parking lot stayed well lit. There was a small drive that led to the back of the strip mall. He took it. The back was the same as the Food Lion, dark with only small lights illuminating the area from above the doors. There were, however, no fenced-in areas. He figured that the air-conditioning units must all be on the roof. The road was narrow and small, and then what was left of the woods beyond that. There was only one way to do this he thought, and this time he would park down the street. He drove back to the front and down the street for about two blocks.

He climbed out of the truck and looked around. It was quiet except for the spiny legs in the back of his cab scraping against the metal that was foreign to them. *Hang on buddies, just a little longer.* He had read that lobsters could survive out of water half a day, so he had a few hours.

Danny grabbed his bag of tools and this time took the sledgehammer. It was heavy and it was about to make a lot of noise. He took up a slow jog and headed for the back of the store. The extra weight caused him to sweat at once.

He tried to conceal the sledgehammer as he approached the shopping mall. There didn't seem to be anyone around. The edge of the remaining woods made for good cover as he walked around to the back. He pulled the mask over his face and pondered his next move.

As he approached the back of the building he figured the back door was his best bet. He got ready to bust down a door, something he had always thought would be exhilarating.

There was a camera here as well, but it was higher and out of his reach. He needed something to stand on. The only things back there were six small trash bins. To get there he would have to run in front of the camera.

He took a deep breath and then charged into the light. As he approached one of the cans, he ran past it before turning around and sliding behind it. The camera, if recording, would only get his back. The bin was on wheels. After catching his breath, he put all his might into the metal bin and moved it under the door. He wasn't sure how much the camera got of him, but now was not the time to think about it. He pulled the paint can from his bag and jumped onto the trash bin. On his tippy toes, Danny again sprayed the lens with paint. He jumped down and caught his breath.

He looked to the door now and tried to assess its strengths. It was made of wood. A good thing he thought. He'd break the doorknob off first and go from there.

Danny set the heavy end of the sledgehammer on the doorknob and let it hold its weight. He judged his distance and decided the arc would be just right.

His heart started racing and he took a few deep breaths. He shuffled his feet to get a good stance. Like an axe man he lifted the mighty hammer a few inches above his target. Then in a swinging motion he let the hammer drop to his feet around in a windmill motion, over his head and down toward his target with all his might. He let out a roar as it came down – then missed. His face panicked. The head of the hammer came down a few inches to the right of its target. It missed and went crashing to the ground in a thunderous explosion. The force and his now awkward stance made the handle pop out of his hands. It bounced up and caught him just under his chin. His head banged into the door and then all was silent.

Danny sat by the backdoor seeing stars. He grabbed for his jaw. It was numb. His mouth filled with saliva and he tried to spit, but most of it trickled onto the front of his shirt. *Well, that sucked.*

He was full of adrenaline and stood back up like a prizefighter that had just been knocked to the ground. He spit again and wiped his mouth. Again he picked up the hammer and lowered it just above the doorknob and adjusted his feet once more. *Here goes nothing.* Again, he let the hammer drop down and around, over his head and down with all his might.

The metal-on-metal explosion was loud. The handle broke off and bounced off the ground. Like a crazed animal he repeatedly swung the hammer sideways, right where the dead bolt was, trying to crush the door inward. With each thundering hit the door started to split. After five crushing blows he broke in.

He was sweating and out of breath. He needed a break, but the noise was back. Same sound. Same alarm. He dropped the hammer and ran into the building.

It was basically the same layout as before, only this one was larger with super high ceilings. He looked for the swinging door and ran for it.

He searched for a grocery cart as he ran but didn't see one. He needed a container on wheels. He stopped and looked around. There was a large container on wheels made of cloth. It looked like it held dirty towels for laundry. He ran toward it. It was full. He was in a rush so he just turned it over on its side and let the towels dump out themselves. He lifted it back up and pushed it toward the swinging doors. Once in, he looked for the seafood section. It wasn't in the middle and at the back like the others.

He cursed himself and again wished he had scoped out the place first. To the right was the milk. He went the other way. He saw the tank all the way down to the left of the massive store. His heavy breathing was beginning to get the best of him. *I am out of shape.*

The only thing that really kept his pace up was the tank he saw ahead. The alarm inside the store wasn't as loud as in the back, but it kept him aware of what he was doing.

The tank was practically full with stacks and stacks of lobsters. Water again splashed everywhere as Danny pulled out them out. It was harder to put them in the laundry bin and slowed him down profusely. He was taking too long. He paused, out of breath, and thought about leaving.

He looked into the eyes of a lobster at the bottom of the tank and immediately got back to work. It took five minutes to empty the tank. He was spent. Again he left his mark on the tank.

Then his adrenaline sensed a new noise, and his heart rate doubled. In the distance he heard sirens. Sirens on cars. Sirens on cop cars.

I took too long. He thought about the lobsters that he might not be able to save, and got a new burst of energy. He pushed the cart and ran as fast as he possibly could. This time he went through some different doors. The alarm now inside the building was too loud for him to hear how far away the cops were.

I am such an idiot. He cursed himself for not going home after the first heist. *Greedy.* They were coming for him and they were most likely pissed. He could be in bed now, enjoying his freedom. Instead, he was about to be handcuffed and brought to jail.

He approached the back door and peered his head out. *Nobody.* He picked up his sledgehammer and gently set it over the lobsters. His instinct told him not to leave it behind. The damn thing had the *Home Depot* written on it anyway. They would surely look to see what dumbass had bought one that same day. He was beginning to panic. This was not working out the way he had planned.

With no time to stop and think about it he pushed the bin toward the door. It didn't fit. *Shit.* The top wire frame was wider than the door. He had no time to look for a different door so he leaned over the lobsters, grabbed the wire, and squeezed it together with all his might. He shuffled his body around and once again tried to push it through the door. He practically popped out into the back drive.

He heard sirens and they were loud. They were at the front of the building already. He swore he could hear voices. Terror overtook him as he saw white car lights and colored flashing lights bouncing off the trees. They were headed to the back.

He pushed the cart down the back drive toward the center of the shopping mall. The lights were approaching. The sirens were getting louder. He was out of time.

Danny grabbed the sledgehammer and started to swing in circles with it. He let go of it sending it into the woods. He then pulled the canvas bag off the wire-framed cart and twisted the top shut. Then he swung the bag and let momentum swing it onto his back. The sound of crunching lobsters sickened him, but there was nothing else he could do. He ran for the woods toward the darkness.

He didn't look back but heard a few cars screech to a halt at his shattered door. He heard voices and car doors closing. He ran. He ran bent over. The lobsters were pushing his bag of tools into his kidneys. It hurt, but he didn't slow down. He took an angle that seemed right for his truck.

It was dark. The twigs breaking below his feet seemed too loud. He kept running. His foot caught under a large branch that he hadn't seen and once again he went crashing to the ground. The bag flew over his head and bent his arm awkwardly. He held his grip. No way was he losing lobsters in these black woods.

His arm ached as he got a better grip and stood back up. He was deep into the woods and thankfully didn't see any flashlights coming his way. He spit out some dirt.

The bag was heavy over his back as he continued his escape. A streetlight ahead broke the darkness. It gave him a second wind. He was close – so close. He came out of the woods about fifty yards from his truck. His legs burned, but he couldn't slow now – so close. He hobbled toward his truck.

Any minute now a cop car could come around the corner and bust him. The thought of a hard concrete floor in a jail cell gave him energy. The last twenty-five yards he felt as if he were flying. Without stopping, he flung the bag again and let the momentum swing into the back of the cab. He felt a hundred pounds lighter, yet he could hardly breathe. He had overdone it.

Exhaustion set in deeply. His muscles cramped up and his stomach ached. He couldn't get enough air and felt queasy. He stumbled to get the keys out of his pocket and dropped them on the ground. He scooped them up and crashed hard into the driver's seat. His hands shook so violently for a moment he didn't think he would find the ignition. The key finally went in.

He cranked twice and threw up in his lap and all over the steering wheel. The holes in his muffler made his truck louder than most vehicles. This brought him back to his senses. He grasped the slimy steering wheel, threw the truck in drive and pulled away. He could hardly drive, but for the second time in one day *The Shellfish Saint* had struck.

CHAPTER 17

THE CAPER HAD happened too late to be in the next morning's paper, but when Danny awoke he knew that he would be on the six o'clock evening news.

Last night had been insane. I need to be smarter or I'm gonna get caught. He turned in the bed slowly. He was hurting. There were scrapes up and down his arms, a bump on his head and under his chin. His ribs felt as if he had been in a fight, and lost.

There was a knock at the door. It was loud. *I thought I told him about knocking like that.* He turned again and grabbed his cell. It was two p.m. There were also two missed calls from Kenny.

His phone rang in his hand, giving him a jolt. It was Kenny. He then heard Kenny's voice at the door.

"Hello," his voice cracked from not being awake yet.

"Danny! Where the hell are you? Are you here?"

"Yeah, give me a sec. Let me just get dressed." He heard Kenny hang up. He paused for a minute. His pillow called back to him. A yawn crept out of him from deep within. He hadn't slept this late in a long time. By the time he had gotten all the lobsters out of the truck, it must have been five a.m. It was as if he were hung-over.

Danny slowly rose and put on some clothes. His arms looked terrible so he pulled a long sleeve t-shirt out of the closet. He shuffled his feet to let Kenny in.

The back door squeaked like his bones, "Hey, man." he let Kenny in and turned to find his coffee maker.

Kenny followed him inside, "What's going on? I've been calling you all day. You were acting really funny yesterday."

"I'm fine, Kenny, really." He put a coffee bag in the coffeemaker and added five heaping, glorious capfuls of crushed coffee beans.

"Did you just wake up? Danny, you gotta get a hold of this. You slept all day? You gotta pick yourself up. Move on."

Confused, Danny looked out the window to the pool as he filled the coffee pot with water and then added it to the coffee machine. He turned it on and then turned to Kenny, "You want some coffee?"

"No, man. I want to talk to you. What can I do? She's gone man. It's been a couple of weeks. You gotta get your head right."

This angered Danny a little, but also made him smile when he realized Kenny thought he sat around the house all day doing nothing. "You remember how I proposed to her? With the lobster and all?"

"Yes, man. Talk to me."

"Well . . ." Danny really didn't know how to say this, "It was embarrassing. When I think about it now, it's the embarrassment that bothers me the most."

"Come on man, you'll never see those people again. Everyone has been dumped. It's nothing to be embarrassed about." Kenny was grabbing at anything, trying to be of help to his friend.

Danny sighed, "Can I just finish?"

"Please, sorry. What happened?"

"Well, when I saw all the eyes just staring at me . . . I ran." He laughed at the thought of himself escaping; finally he could laugh about it, "I just ran, Kenny."

"I heard. She told Stephanie and she feels really bad about it. She wants—"

"If you keep interrupting, I'm not gonna finish the story."

"There's more?"

This made Danny laugh really loud, "Uhh . . . yeah, there's one little extra teeny tiny thing that I did, or am doing, or I *did.*"

Kenny went to speak but stayed silent to hear what he had to say. The timer on the coffee broke in.

Danny grabbed his worn coffee cup out of the sink and filled it full. "You sure you don't want a cup?"

"NO, MAN! What teeny tiny thing did you do, are you doing? Why is your chin cut?" Kenny answered, frustrated.

This wasn't going to be easy, and a visual might help. "Let's go outside," Danny walked to the door, "I need some fresh air." Kenny followed as they walked toward the pool.

Danny continued, "So there I am running to the front door and it was blocked with eyes, so without stopping I turned and ran the other way, passed more eyes."

"Okay, that is pretty bad."

"You have no idea. I'll never forget Stacy's face as she looked at me in horror. She was as embarrassed as me, yet when I ran she froze. So, I ran past her, past the kitchen staff and through the kitchen."

"You escaped through the kitchen? Just like in the movies?" Kenny tried to help with some humor.

"Yes. Just like the movies." they shared a smile. "So as I'm running through the kitchen, I see the lobster just sitting there, about to be boiled. The kitchen was empty now, because all the eyes were out in the dining room." They had reached the edge of the pool. Wrapped up in the story, Kenny had yet to take his eyes off of Danny.

"So what did you do?"

Here goes, "I grabbed Stacy's lobster and made a break for it."

Kenny stared at him blankly. "You stole Stacy's lobster?"

"Yes."

Kenny forced a laugh, "That's it? You stole a lobster? That's the big thing you've been wanting to tell me?" Kenny was clearly confused by this anticlimactic story.

"Well," Danny spoke slowly, "That's not exactly all of it." He had a mischievous smile on his face.

"What?"

"I've kind of . . ." he spoke and nodded his head toward the pool.

Kenny's eyes followed his. He jumped back – first, because he wasn't used to seeing the pool drained; and second, for what was under the water.

Danny was a little shocked as well. Last night's catch had really added to the numbers.

"Danny . . . what have you done? Where did you get these?"

This was it, Danny thought. Kenny was either going to get it or not get it. "I am . . . *The Shellfish Saint*," he spoke with pride and pointed to his lobsters.

"The what? Did you steal all these lobsters? Danny, from where? They're going to lock you up," Kenny sputtered with near shock.

"Now, just hang on there. I've been very careful," he lied.

"Answer me. Where did you get these?" Kenny's voice was rising.

"Mostly from . . . uh . . . grocery stores." Danny cleared his throat.

"Grocery stores? Oh God. We have to get rid of these. If anyone sees this, you'll be arrested!" Kenny was *not* getting it.

"Did you know lobsters feel *pain?*" He tried to defend himself, "And they can live to be over a hundred!"

"Who cares!" Kenny screamed.

"EXACTLY!" Danny screamed louder. "Nobody cares! That's just it. We stack these amazing creatures four deep in fish tanks and then boil them . . . ALIVE! Why does no one see the absurdity of that?"

"Absurdity?" Kenny was clearly shaken. "Absurdity! Your pool is full of lobsters that you *stole*! That's absurdity! She has really messed with your head, man. Lobsters can't even live in *chlorine* pools Danny. Did you think of that?"

"That's not chlorine. We emptied it and then we put in some salt water. And this isn't about her," he said, trying more to convince himself than Kenny. "Don't you—"

"We? Who's we?" Kenny questioned.

"Brad is helping me take care of them. Will you just relax?"

"What! You've involved Brad? He's just a kid, but they'll arrest him too! What were you thinking? This is crazy Danny. You have to snap out of it, before something bad happens."

"Something bad is happening!" Danny snapped back. "Every day, all over the world, man is torturing innocent creatures!"

Kenny moved his arms erratically. "You've lost it, Danny. This must be some kind of post-break-up syndrome. You need to talk to someone. You need help."

"You need to leave," Danny said in a calm voice. Kenny didn't get it.

Kenny shook his head, "Danny, I can't let you do this to yourself."

Danny seized him by the collar hard, "You better not tell a soul, you hear me! Especially not that big-mouth wife of yours." He didn't mean to say that. It just came out of his mouth.

Kenny slowly grabbed Danny's hand and pulled it off of him. He turned and walked to his car. Danny wanted to say sorry, but the words escaped him. Kenny got in his car and left, never making eye contact with him. Danny threw his coffee mug against the house smashing it into pieces. "Damn it!" he screamed.

Eyes. He felt eyes again. He looked over and saw Brad's dad looking out the window. *Great*, he thought. He wondered how much he had heard. Danny decided that he wasn't going to tell anyone else his secret. He hoped Brad would do the same.

He spent the rest of the day indoors. He needed the seclusion. The small TV in the kitchen was on to distract him. He thought he'd pay some bills, but he just sat and stared. He hated what he'd said to Kenny. Kenny deserved better than that. He just didn't understand. Of all people, he needed Kenny to understand. Maybe it was just the fear of what would happen if he got caught that set Kenny off. Kenny cared and Danny knew that.

He got up and decided to clean the counter and catch up on some dishes. His ski mask was on the counter. He picked it up and thought about last night's events. He rubbed the bump on his head. *The lobsters need someone to stand up for them. They need me, or has she just made me crazy.* He felt in his heart that he was doing right and that was enough for him. If Kenny didn't understand, well that was his problem.

Danny looked out to the pool. It was a sanctuary, and he saw one of its trusty loyalists walk by and wave. Danny waved back. Brad had a new bag of shrimp, which he raised proudly. Danny waited for him to look into the pool.

Brad did and dropped the bag. He raised his hands to Danny in amazement. Danny laughed and just raised his shoulders jokingly.

Then, the voice on the TV caught him. The local news was on. The anchorwoman spoke, "Next, we're gonna go out to Robert Starnes who is doing a follow-up to a story you may have seen last week. Robert?"

The camera cut to Robert who was on the scene. Danny recognized the seafood section of the store. It was missing its lobsters.

"Thanks, Jessica. Well, folks, *The Shellfish Saint* has struck again," Robert said with a smirk, "This is the same scene as the other *two* grocery stores."

Danny pounded on the window and motioned for Brad to come quickly. Brad dropped the bag and ran inside. "What's up?"

Danny just motioned to the TV.

"I say two, because two grocery stores were hit last night," Robert was explaining.

Danny looked to Brad and raised his eyebrows.

"This is Paul." The camera widened to get both men in the shot, "Paul is the store manager. What did they take sir?"

The camera made Paul nervous. He spoke fast and loud, "The lobsters. They took all the lobsters." He stared right into the camera, nervous.

The reporter questioned, "Did they take anything else?"

"No, sir. The lobsters. They took all the lobsters."

"Why do you think they would just take the lobsters?"

"Don't know. Hungry, I guess."

The camera moved back to Robert the reporter as he walked up to the tank. "I don't think whoever it is intends to eat them. The word Saint implies savior."

Brad patted Danny on the back. Danny smiled. He was glad Brad understood.

"It appears someone or some animal rights group is on a quest to rescue lobsters. Why else would they sign it, *The Shellfish Saint?*" Robert asked.

Jessica cut in, "They do meet with an awful ending. Being boiled."

Robert quickly jumped in, "Yes, well. I know a lot of people, my father included, who make a living off them, so it's no laughing matter. *This Shellfish Saint* or whoever they are, need to be caught. The police are asking that if you have any leads or see any suspicious activity, to please call them immediately. I'm Robert Starnes reporting for *Bay Nine News.*"

"Okay, thanks, Robert." The camera cut back to Jessica and the other anchor, "Animal activists for lobsters?"

"Yes," Jessica added. "Interesting story. In other news, the water department—"

Danny turned off the TV. He looked to Brad. "Did you know eating lobsters is a two billion dollar a year industry?"

"Two billion?" Brad added, "Maybe you should leave some paperwork about it. Didn't you say you read that tests proved lobsters feel pain?"

"Yes, they do."

"Get that reporter to read that on the air and maybe some people will join your cause."

"Not with his dad a lobster fisherman," Danny said. "Mr. Robert Starnes seemed a little angry."

"Well, whatever you do, the cat's out of the bag, now. You better be careful."

"I know. No more grocery stores for awhile." "You hit two last night? What's it like?"

"It was terror, especially the second one. The cops were there before I was far enough away. I'll never forget their voices over the walkie-talkies. They were so close, too close, man. I was rough on the lobsters too. I thought for sure I would find some floating today."

"I didn't see any. They are well fed too, man."

"Yeah. Thanks, man. I worry you're getting too close. If the cops ever come here, you make sure you say you were never here."

"Alright, man. Don't worry about me. You just play it smart and keep them from finding this place. It'd be a shame for all the lobsters to have to go back to the tanks."

Danny shook his head, "Agreed. That would not be good."

"So, what's next?"

"I think I'll try to get some by the pier as they come in. There are a couple of places that receive them right off the boat." He didn't tell Brad about the girl he met. It was probably all in his head anyway. Maybe she was just bored and looking for conversation.

"All right, bro. Let me know if you need anything. And get some sleep. You look old. I mean you *are* old; now you look *really* old."

Danny threw a dishtowel at him. "Did your father say anything about me and Kenny screaming at each other earlier?"

"Nah, man. Me and Dad don't talk much. Kenny knows?"

"Yeah, and he wasn't happy. Especially when he found out you knew. He's right, though, you should keep your distance."

Brad stood defiantly, "What? That pool is my sanctuary too. And now that I can't swim in it, I might as well help feed them. I'll holla at cha later."

"Yeah, I'll holla too," Danny said, trying to fit it. Brad just shook his head.

"Give it up man. Later."

"Later . . . dude."

Chapter 18

DANNY LAID LOW for a few days. One, to let things settle down; and two, his body needed to heal. By Monday he was getting antsy, so he decided it was time for another rescue.

He gathered all his tools and readied the black outfit. He was going to rob *her* place and he wasn't sure how he felt about it. Yesterday, he'd purchased a crowbar, two large laundry bags, and also a replacement lock and dead bolt. He would leave that for her. It cost sixty dollars, and money was something he was running low on. Being *The Shellfish Saint* was getting to be expensive.

When the truck was packed he waited until after midnight. He didn't notice any cameras when he was there but brought the paint just in case. He was learning to expect the unexpected.

He drove around to the back of the store. He'd decided he had to park right at the back door because there would be no grocery carts to transport them in. The street only had a few lights on it. It looked relatively quiet. Across the street was a different story. It was lined with houses. He would have to keep the noise level down.

He was wearing an eye patch. Something he learned from watching *Mythbusters* and now he was going to see if it worked.

He pulled around back and silently got out and eased the door shut. Softly, he put on his bag, and grabbed the crow bar. All was quiet.

He approached the back door. A security light came on. He froze. He'd expected that, but the brightness that was now giving him away made him uneasy. He figured he would stand still at the door until the light went back out. So he did. It was a long forty-five seconds.

When the light went out, he went to work instantly. The door was old, as was the frame. He gently pressed the tip of the crowbar into the space between the door and frame. He paused. Still quiet. He pushed slowly on the crow bar and the wood began to splinter. He took a deep breath. He couldn't be too loud. He pressed again. It slowly splintered and popped like burning firewood. The wood was old and gave little resistance to the steel of the crow bar. He pulled the replacement lock out and set it by the door so as not to forget when leaving.

He entered. It was dark. Pitch black. He couldn't see a thing. Danny pulled the eye patch over to the other eye, and, damn if it didn't work. Apparently, pirates wore eye patches when they raided ships for a reason. When they went down into the darkened hull, the covered eye would already be adjusted to the dark and could see much better than one fresh from the light. It worked on *Mythbusters* when they tried and it was working now for the Shellfish Saint. He had walked halfway into the store before realizing he hadn't grabbed the flashlight out of his bag. He didn't need it.

He eased his way into the store. Water pumps made a lot of noise. It worried him. Someone could walk in behind him and he wouldn't hear them. He decided to move a little faster.

There were large coolers in the back. Probably holding all the frozen fish. It smelled of dead sea life. He used to love the smell of these places but now was saddened by it. It reinforced why he was here. There was fresh air back at his sanctuary, and life.

He reached the tank that held the lobsters and unplugged the pump so he could see the bottom better. There were quite a few. They would fill both laundry bags.

He didn't hesitate and started filling the bags with bound-clawed lobsters. He thought of them as he pulled them out. The helplessness they must feel. Their only means of defense, besides the hard shell, were their claws. In half a second, humans could render them useless with a rubber band. He wondered if they bonded with each other, since they were all in the same unfortunate situation. But now the Shellfish Saint was here.

He grabbed the last one. The tank was not on the ground, so he just signed the wall and then he exited.

So far, so good. He placed the bags on the ground and slowly opened the door. He exited backward, pulling the bags, and then gently let the door close.

He turned to the truck and there she was – the girl from the store. The girl from *this* store, leaning up against his truck as if she were picking him up from school.

His gut hurt. He wanted to run, but couldn't move. They just stared at each other for a few beats.

"*You're* the Shellfish Saint?" she asked mockingly.

"I . . ." he had no idea what to say. The situation was clear though. He was busted. *The lock. Tell her about the lock.*

She continued first, "I was just sitting there in my room; that's my house right there, my room's the second on the right there. When I saw the light come on over here. Now I had just gotten home from a club and was a little buzzed, but I thought, I know that light never comes on, 'cause people don't come back here after closing."

"Listen, I—"

"So I look out the window," apparently she wasn't finished, "and I see you. The guy who practically ran away from me the other day."

"Can I just explain?"

She ignored him and finished her story, "So, I thought to myself, well, this is cute; he's gonna leave me flowers or a note by the back door, or some other romantic gesture. But now, why is he wearing that eye patch, I wondered?" She looked right at him.

He took it off, embarrassed.

"But then you took out a crow bar and broke into my daddy's store. So, I risked my life, instead of calling the police, and came over here to see why you broke into my daddy's store. Are you dangerous, mister?"

"Mister? No . . . No. My name is Danny, and—"

Still not finished, she continued, "Then I remember watching the TV and seeing about someone who was going around town stealing lobsters. I thought, isn't that just the silliest thing you ever heard. So what do you have to say for yourself?"

Danny hesitated, "First . . . let me just say," now he wished she'd kept talking, because he had no idea what to say.

"Cat's got your tongue? And you got my daddy's lobsters."

"I'm sorry. I left a new lock there for you. Really, I don't—"

"You better do better than that, Danny boy," she taunted. "I'm risking my life here. A lobster thief is obviously dangerous."

He thought he heard a laugh from her.

"You need to tell me why I don't call the police right now," she was holding her cell in her hand like a gun. And she was about to shoot him down. "Or worse yet, tell me why I don't wake up my daddy and tell him—"

"Please!" The word burst out of his mouth, "I'm not dangerous. I'll put them back and I left a new lock there because of you. I thought you were cute the other day, and that's why—"

"That's why you ran from me?"

"I know. I'm sorry. I felt like a fool for the rest of the day. Guess I've lost a step or something." He shook his shoulders, dejected.

"You're about to lose your freedom, if you don't give me a good logical reason for your thievery."

"I don't know what to say," he wanted her to understand.

"How about the truth," she said, plainly.

So he told her . . . the truth. Why not, he had nothing to lose. He spoke fast and in one breath, "Two weeks ago I proposed to my girlfriend. I took her to the restaurant where we had our first date. She loves lobsters."

"She makes you steal lobsters?"

"No. She . . . can I just finish?"

"I'm all ears," she crossed her arms. She seemed to be enjoying this.

He took a breath, "I had them put the ring around one of the live lobsters that are in the tank at the front door. Have you ever been to *The Fisherman's Shack?*"

"I'm familiar with the place."

"Well we walk up to the tank and there is the ring shining as bright as a diamond can. She saw it. I thought she was speechless from happiness, so I got on one knee in front of everyone in the restaurant and popped the question. You know what she said?"

"First, you have to steal me all the lobsters?" she said with a smirk.

His face became blank, "She said we have to talk."

Her smile left. She paused before speaking, "You were on your knee and she gave you the 'we have to talk' line?"

"Yes," he looked to the ground and shook his head.

"What did you do?" she asked quietly.

He fought back his emotion, "I ran."

"You *ran?*" she prompted, moving a little closer to him.

"Yes. And it was no quick escape. The front door was blocked with onlookers."

"Oh, dear heavens," she covered her mouth, feeling his pain.

"So I ran the other way; past her, past the kitchen staff. There was no place to go through except the kitchen."

"You left through the kitchen?"

"Yep. And that's where I saw her lobster. Just sitting there, waiting to be boiled for my special occasion. So, I grabbed her and ran out the back." He paused for a moment, "And well, you've seen the rest on TV, I guess."

She left the truck and walked right up to him, "Did you sign the wall in there?"

"Yes. Sorry, I—"

"Let me see your pen?"

"What?"

"Your pen. Let me see your pen."

He pulled the marker out of his pocket and gave it to her.

She looked hard into his eyes, "Now let me see your hand."

Confused, he offered it to her. She turned it over and started writing on his palm, "My name is Becca. That is the saddest story I've ever heard." She paused and looked at him, "They were blocking the front door?"

He just shook his head up and down. She let go of his hands and grabbed one of the bags beside him and continued to the truck. "The way I see it, Danny boy, you owe me a dinner to explain why in the hell you were wearing an eye patch." she stopped and turned to him, "Think you can handle that?"

She's letting me go? "Yes," he quickly said. "Yes. I think I can handle that . . . Becca."

"Good." She continued to the truck and placed the bag in the back,

"I'll give you a few days to think about it." She headed across the street and never looked back.

He sat there for a moment and then looked at his hand, at her phone number. *Who is this person?* He thought.

Danny grabbed the other bag, and placed it into the back. He climbed into the driver's side and quietly shut the door. Before cranking the truck, he looked to her house. She had already gone inside. He shook his head and smiled. *Becca.*

CHAPTER 19

DANNY SPENT THE next day thinking about Becca. Why had she let him go? He owed her now, and he wasn't sure that was a good thing.

It was late afternoon, and he had the TV on waiting to see if his story was developing. He had paced the room, anxious about getting caught. He retraced his steps and felt safe about any fingerprints. Becca knowing his identity made him uneasy.

Brad knocked and opened the door at the same time. He went straight for the fridge. Brad was almost like family and knew he didn't have to ask if he could raid the kitchen.

"Did you go out last night?" Brad asked casually, his back to him.

Danny laughed, "Yeah, you could say that."

Brad could tell in his voice something had happened, and his interest grew, "More excitement? Guess we're waiting for the news?"

"I got busted last night," Danny said, not looking away from the TV.

"What!" shouted Brad, racing to the TV.

"Yep. Caught red-handed. Right in the thick of it. My hand was in the cookie jar."

"Uhh, they didn't lock you up?" Brad questioned, confused. "They just let you go?"

"*She* let me go," Danny said quietly.

Brad hesitated and then asked, "She let you go? Who is *she?*"

"Becca." Danny gave him a quick look and a smile, then took a sip from a bottled beer.

"Who's Becca, Danny?" Brad laughed as Danny was clearly amused by this all.

"She works the register for her dad at Fresh Ed's. I decided the grocery stores would be watched, so I figured no one would be looking down by the pier. I was wrong." he took another sip.

A jingle on the TV alerted them that the news was about to start.

"Good evening everyone, I'm Jessica Ashley. He's back. The Shellfish Saint has struck again, and this time it wasn't a grocery store. Robert Starnes has the story. Robert?"

"Thanks, Jessica. I'm out here by the Washington Pier and yes the lobster thief has struck again." Danny noticed he didn't say *Shellfish Saint*, and his pulse began to race.

"I'm here with the family who owns Fresh Ed's." he walked a few feet and there she was with Ed and right behind her a woman, Danny concluded this was her mother. The *Fresh Ed's* sign was just over their shoulder.

"That's her!" Danny shouted.

Brad leaned closer for a better look, "That's Becca? Does she know your name? She's gonna rat you out on TV!"

Robert stuck the microphone in front of her face, "Can you tell us what happened?"

Becca spoke for the family, "Well, we came in and opened the store just like any other day, and written right on the wall was The Shellfish Saint was here. I watch the news so I knew about the story. I knew they took our lobsters."

"She said they," interjected Brad relieved. Danny could see she was acting and knew she wouldn't tell. His pulse slowed.

"How did they get in?" Robert asked.

"Through the back door. It was cracked right open. Must have used a crowbar or something to pry it open."

"This is serious criminal activity folks and no laughing matter. This town lives off selling seafood. And this is becoming a liability. You'll have to replace the door I suppose," he pushed the microphone ahead again.

"Well not all of it," Becca said to the camera. Danny wasn't sure how she was keeping a straight face.

"What do you mean?" asked the reporter.

"They left a new lock set by the back door for us."

Robert looked back into the camera, "It seems this *Shellfish Saint* is trying to be a modern day Robin Hood. There seems to be more to this story than we currently have, Jessica."

"They left a new lock for them?" Jessica asked, surprised.

"It appears so, Jessica."

"Okay, thanks, Robert. What is the public's reaction to all this?"

"Well, Jessica, that's just what we're going to find out. If I can get the camera to follow me." They started walking down the pier and they came up to a man in his forties.

"Excuse me, sir. I was wondering if you had heard about this *Shell-fish Saint*?"

The man looked at the mic and then the camera, "Yeah, I heard he's stealing things."

"Lobsters," Robert clarified. "He has been stealing lobsters from grocery stores and just last night from *Fresh Ed's*. What are your thoughts on that?"

"Well I grew up on this pier, and I know Ed and his family well. They are good hard working people. So, they need to catch this guy."

"Can I ask you sir, do you eat lobster?"

"Yes I do. Love lobster."

"Any issues with them being boiled alive?" he pushed the mic closer.

"Ahh, hell – sorry," the man apologized to the camera. "Heck. You can't do nothing these days without someone wanting to protest you."

Robert smirked, "Thank you for your time." Danny thought Robert was happy with the man's response.

Two elderly men approached to see what all the fuss was about.

Danny laughed, "Oh man, it's Larry and Andy. They'll call for my head."

Robert noticed them and went right for them, "Excuse me, any thoughts on this *Shellfish Saint*?"

"Is that what this is about?" questioned Larry. "I tell you what, you bring that thief down here and me and the boys will take care of it."

Danny saw Mildred in the background. She was a regular at the bar, too, but mostly kept to herself. Robert, sensing Larry would start cursing on live TV, moved away. It all felt surreal to Danny who wasn't used to seeing people he knew on TV.

"Hello, ma'am. We're trying to get the public's thoughts on this *Shellfish Saint*." he pressed the microphone forward.

She paused for a moment from all the attention. Robert pried further, "Any thoughts on this?"

"Well," she looked at the camera, "I'm not one to cause a fuss, but I think boiling anything that is alive is just plain wrong."

"YES!" Brad screamed at the TV. "You tell them, lady!"

Robert seemed to pull the microphone back, but Mildred pursued the subject. "Not that I think stealing is right, mind you, but have you ever seen the conditions they are subjected to? They pile them right on top of each other; almost looks like they can't move at all."

Robert took back control, "Well, that about does it here, Jessica. Looks like the majority of the people here want to see some justice."

"Well, keep us posted, Robert. Looks like she wanted some justice for the lobsters?" She looked over to her co-anchor, "Are you opposed to cooking lobsters live?"

"I've never really thought about it. I've heard they don't feel pain."

The camera went back to Jessica, "We'll need to research that and get some facts. Wendy has the weather for us. Is the rain coming?"

Brad turned off the TV. "I guarantee you ask any creature what it's like to be boiled alive, and they'll all say the same thing – No thanks!"

Danny thought of what he had heard on the TV. "Some of them were really pissed at me, though."

"Well, that's their fault," Brad rose to leave. "I'll talk to you later. Mom's cooking spaghetti for me tonight. Later."

"Later." Danny was glad Brad had plans. He had plans of his own. Becca had given him a few days to think it over – he didn't need them. He wanted to talk to her.

CHAPTER 20

DANNY HAD PROGRAMMED her number into his phone the night she gave it to him. Now he had to dial it, and that was proving to be a little harder.

What if she were setting him up? His little voice told him she wasn't. They had that energy between them. He felt he had known her for years. He would have been excited to call her, except for the elephant in the room, or rather lobster.

He set the phone on the kitchen counter and took a beer out of the fridge. He took a big gulp. Two big gulps. *Okay, I'll drink one beer and then call her.*

He decided he'd be more comfortable out by the pool, so he took his beer and phone and headed outside. The sun was closing up shop for the night, so he turned the pool light on to see them better. He had quite the catch now and admired them from above.

Funny how fast life can change, he thought. *One minute you're diving into a pool, the next you're putting lobsters into it.* If people didn't get it, he didn't care. They needed his help, and he had all the time in the world for them now. Besides, here they didn't have to sit right on top of each other.

Feeling confident, he just picked up the phone and dialed her number without thinking of what to say. He said hello out loud a few times to test his voice and make sure it didn't crack.

"Hello," she said.

"Hel . . ." it cracked. He cleared his throat and tried again, "Hello, uh, Becca. Hi, it's Danny."

"Sorry, you must have the wrong number."

He gasped audibly. Had she given him a bogus number? He sat up straight and knocked the empty beer bottle into the pool.

"I'm kidding, Danny," she said cheerfully.

"Ahh," he laughed, "How are you?"

"I'm good. Did you see me on the news tonight?"

"I did. . . ." *Compliment her.* "You're very good on camera."

"Really? I felt like I was mumbling through the whole thing. My friends have been calling me all night. Seems you've turned me into a bit of a celebrity."

He didn't like the sound of her friends all calling. Would she tell them, and then they would tell someone and then everyone would know.

She noticed his silence, "Don't worry, Danny boy, I haven't told a soul. Have you?"

He lied, "Me? No. Keeping this one kind of close to home, if you know what I mean."

"That's probably smart. My daddy is pissed."

The way she talked about her dad made him feel old. His dad would be pissed too though and would probably turn him in to teach him a lesson.

"You still there?" she asked.

"Yeah. Sorry. So . . . Becca deserves a dinner."

"That she does."

"Any place in particular that she would like to go?"

"I was thinking seafood."

He paused and then they both started laughing. "Well, any place you want to go, any time."

"Okay, how about Italian? Giovanni's?"

"Sounds great."

"Meet you there at 8:30?"

The crack in his voice was back, "Tonight?"

"No time like the present, Danny boy, unless you already got plans tonight – with your eye patch."

He half laughed, and then coughed, "Nah, that's cool. I can do 8:30."

"See you then then," she hung up.

Danny looked down into the pool. *She wants to have dinner tonight.*

Chapter 21

Danny didn't want to be late, so he showered early. The youth had come out in him when he realized he tried on three shirts, settling on a solid color and keeping it casual with some jeans. *Shoes or sandals?* He went with shoes.

He arrived at Giovanni's at 8:15 and asked for a table for two. He hadn't been in a restaurant since the incident and hadn't thought about all the eyes that would be there. The host was going to put them in the middle of the dining room, until Danny saw a small square table in the corner. "How about that one?"

"Sure thing." She sat him and took away two place settings, leaving two side by side, and then set down two menus. He wondered if he should move the other place setting so she would sit across from him. He didn't.

"Can I get you anything while you wait?"

"Yes, can I see the wine list, please," there needed to be a little buzz in the air tonight.

"Oh it's right here," she had already set it down.

"Ahh, sorry." He quickly opened it and went straight for the Pinot. *Not the cheapest, not the most expensive. That one.* "Can we get a bottle of the Sonoma Pinot, please?"

"Sure, I'll be right back."

A few minutes later she returned with a bottle and two glasses, "Shall I let it breathe?"

"Please," he said and checked his watch.

She opened the bottle and then handed him the cork. She then poured a taste into his glass. For some reason he never quite felt comfortable with this ritual. Maybe it was issues with his dad, but deciding on the wine always made him feel out of place. He tasted and said perfect, just as he always did. He knew the basics. Merlot was a little sweet and Cab a little dry. Maybe it was because he loved any Pinot, cheap or expensive. He had never sent one back. She filled a little more in his glass and then the other. She smiled and left.

"Thank you," Danny said. He looked around and then took a slightly larger sip than normal. He felt excited, yet wondered if she was out to set him up. He checked his watch and took one more sip.

She arrived at 8:45. She had made him wait. He was more than anxious at this point, but the wine was settling in. He had to refill his glass to make it look as if he had just arrived as well.

"Sorry I'm late." She swooped her sundress under her as she sat down. She looked great. Her dirty blond hair bounced off her shoulders as she scooted onto her chair. She noticed the wine.

"Ahh, some vino. I feel so grown-up," again she made him feel old.

"Can we get that out of the way then?" Danny questioned, undecided.

"What's that, Danny?" she smiled at him and took a sip.

He paused, knowing he was getting into dangerous territory. "How old are you?"

"Now Danny, you know you never ask a woman that."

Danny looked at her and smiled, "You never ask an *older* woman that."

"Touché," she took another sip of her wine. "Alright then, how old do I look?"

Damn, Danny thought. He better be close. What if she's older than he thinks? That would piss a younger woman off. "Never mind," he said, and took a sip of wine himself, "It's not *that* important."

"Ha ha, nice try, Danny boy. Now you *must* guess."

"Alright," he said, giving her a long look as he squinted his eyes. "Twenty-three," he said quickly and then tilted back his glass.

She nodded, "Not bad. Twenty-two."

"Whoooo," Danny jokingly wiped his brow. He also quickly did the math. He was sixteen years older than her. "I believe I passed the first test, then?" the wine was helping his conversation.

"That you did. Now . . . how old are you?"

Danny laughed out loud, "Ha! Don't you know you never ask an *older* man how old he is."

"Thirty-two?" she jumped in.

"Ouch," he said. "No, Miss Becca. . . ." he put his napkin in his lap, pausing and wondering how she would react to his age. He then looked right in her eyes, "I'm a very comfortable thirty-eight."

"Well, you look great for your age." she said, not embarrassed in the least.

Again, he felt it . . . *for my age?* Like he could keel over at any minute. *Stay focused*, he thought.

"Sixteen is not a bad number, either." She had done the math as well. "It's a complex number," she added and lifted her glass.

The young waiter approached and asked if they were ready to order. *Great*, Danny thought, *competition from the staff.* He was her age and handsome with a mischievous smile on his face. But Becca paid him no mind and kept her eyes on Danny. "I know what I want. Do you need a few minutes?"

"No, I'm ready."

"I'll have the fettuccini. I always get the fettuccini," she said to Danny. "And no salad."

Danny wanted the cheese ravioli but his nervousness took over and he said, "That sounds delicious, I'll have the fettuccini as well."

"Salad?" asked the waiter.

Danny looked shyly to Becca, "Uh, no."

"Very well," the waiter said, "Two fettuccini, no salad." He took the menus and left.

There was a quick lull as they were alone again. She took charge. "So, you were going to tell me about the eye patch. Fashion or function?"

"Function," he said. "Something I caught on Mythbusters."

"Love that show," she quickly added.

"They had an episode about pirate myths. They didn't wear patches over their eyes because they were missing an eye."

"Really?"

"I know. I always figured they lost an eye from a sword fight or something, but in actuality, when they went deep into a darkened hull," – *wait, was that a sexual reference he quickly thought, embarrassed* – "they would switch the patch to the eye that was already adjusted to the dark, and they could see much better."

"Wow, that is crazy," she said.

"You know how they always do tests on that show?"

"Yes."

"Well, they set up a maze of objects. When they turned out the lights they couldn't see a thing. Pitch black. But when they had on the eye patch and moved it, they had no problem seeing where they were going." he took a sip of wine.

"And it works for you as well?" she asked.

"Yeah. It was amazing, . . . " he stopped, realizing it was her store that he had used it on. He wanted to change the subject. "So what about you?"

"What about me?" she teased.

"You're not your everyday seafood . . . dealer, or whatever you call it." Yikes, was the wine making him silly already?

She laughed. *Thank the heavens she laughed.* "Well . . ." she thought about it. "When I'm not *fish dealing*, I am enrolled at the community college, which is okay, but now they want me to declare a major."

"Ahh, the big decision. What does Becca want to be when she grows up?"

"Not *dealing* fish, I can tell you that. I love my mom and daddy, but I swear I was adopted."

Anytime she mentioned her family he felt guilty for stealing from them.

"What about you? Or is being the Shellfish Saint your full-time job?" It really *didn't* seem to bother her.

"Well, I ran a poorly managed dive boat."

She nodded, "That makes sense."

"Which part? The poorly managed or the dive boat?" The wine was loosening him up.

"You're attracted to the underwater world. So you steal lobsters and then return them to their homes. Is that about right?" she asked sipping her wine.

He hesitated. How much should he tell her? "Yeah, about. I haven't *exactly* sent them home yet."

She stared at him, her wine glass in her hand, "Really, well where are they?"

"In my swimming pool," the nonchalant way he said it made them both burst out laughing. He suddenly realized that he liked her. She was easy to talk to, especially under the circumstances. He liked who he was as he talked to her.

"So, no end of the summer pool parties at your house?"

"That's right," he laughed again. "Although, I did see some lobsters handing out fliers the other day," they laughed again. With every laugh he relaxed more in his chair. "Another glass?"

"Sure, why not?"

They were silent as he poured them each a glass. The conversation quickly returned.

"So, did you grow up around here?" she took a sip and asked. He understood. They still had to get the normal first date questions out of the way.

"Yeah, born and raised. You?"

"Go *Seahawks*." she pumped her fist. "You ever thought about leaving?"

His pulse jumped with the flood of memories, "Lately . . . yes."

"Where would you go?"

This made him uncomfortable. This was why Stacy said no. He *didn't* know. He got lost in his thoughts. Where was he going? People his age are well into 'where they're going.' He had nothing to show for his life, except for an old truck and a boat with a for sale sign on it.

"You okay?" she broke in, noticing this had hit a nerve.

Jarred back to their conversation, he said, "Ahh, yes. Sorry."

This was their first awkward moment of the night. A lull took over the table. They both went for their wine glasses. *Say something! Anything.* He suddenly thought he had absolutely nothing to say ever again for the rest of his life.

The waiter showed up with the fettuccini. Danny had never been so happy in his life to see a waiter show up with fettuccini.

"Here we go. Two fettuccines." He set her plate down and then his. "Cheese?" he showed her a block of parmigiana.

"Yes, please."

He grated her some cheese. Danny knew that in a minute the waiter would leave, and he desperately searched his head for a new conversation to start.

"Cheese?" the waiter was talking to him.

"Please. Thanks."

The waiter grated and then stood up. "Can I get you anything else?"

Yes. Would you happen to have any conversation I can use?

After a pause, Becca spoke up, "I think we're good, thanks."

"Very well. Enjoy." He left.

Danny went straight for his food. The mood changed. Why was he nervous?

She twirled some pasta with her fork and spoon and then took a bite. "Mmmmm, wow. That is some lull that just took over."

"What?"

"A lull just took over our table."

Danny laughed, "I know. Sorry."

"Don't be. It was bound to happen. It is up to us to make it go away. See there. I think it just did."

She shrugged her shoulders and twirled some pasta. She was wise for her age. *An old soul*, he thought. *Don't think just talk.*

"I tell you what," she added. "If it comes back, we still haven't talked about the weather."

Danny laughed. She was funny. "Alright, then." He took a bite. "Good call on the fettuccini." He grabbed some more pasta with his fork and twirled with his spoon as well.

"You twirl your pasta well," she flirted.

"Ah, yes. My mother was Italian. She knew her way around the kitchen table."

"That's sweet," Becca added. "My mother, too. I mean, my mother isn't Italian, but she loves to be in the kitchen." The calm returned. "Your mother raised you right. You're a good person, Danny boy. I can tell. That girl was a fool to leave you. Have you talked to her since? I mean does she know you took the lobster?"

Becca was forward. Maybe it was her youth. Danny didn't mind, though. He seemed to like everything about her and wanted to tell her everything. "I haven't talked to her, no. She's friends with my best friend's wife, so they tell her how I am."

"And how is that?" she took a bite.

He squirmed in his chair and cleared his throat, "You sure you want to talk about this? Or better yet, I'm not sure I want to talk about this."

She stared him down, "Don't hold it in Danny. You'll end up stealing lobsters the rest of your life."

That hit a little too close to home. She could see it on his face, "I'm sorry. That was really insensitive of me. Sometimes I just blurt any old thing out of my mouth."

"It's okay," Danny replied. "You're right," they both took sips of wine. Two sips. Three sips. A taste of pasta. Another lull.

"So the heat looks like it's finally breaking," Danny smiled to her.

She laughed in her wine glass, "Yes, but a storm seems to be a brew-in'!"

The waiter showed up, "How is everything?"

"Fantastic," Danny said. His eyes were on hers.

"Very good," the waiter pulled out the check, "I will just leave this for you."

"Okay," Danny responded, his eyes still on hers. It was his time to ask some questions. "So . . . no boyfriend for Becca?"

"No," she smiled, "Got my first broken heart this summer."

He just met this girl, but genuinely felt bad for her, "Ahh, sorry. How long were you together?"

"Three years of high school. He went off to college inland. I stayed here. We tried the long distance thing, but he didn't come home for summer, and decided to get a job there and an apartment with his frat brothers. Michael was his name. Bastard gave me my first broken heart."

"It's true what they say," added Danny. He raised his glass. "The first cut is the deepest."

"Really?" Becca inquired, "You still remember your first broken heart?"

"I'm not that old! And yes I do. Her name was Tracy. My first real love. Met her my freshman year. We were inseparable, first time away from home. We spent every night together for seven months," he savored a sip of his wine, "She was something else."

"What happened?"

"She went home to see her family one weekend. She drove a white Mazda RX-7." Danny smiled to Becca and shook his head, "She was hot in that car. Anyway, she comes back and we go out for dinner one night. I go up to open the passenger door and I see it. . . ." he paused for effect.

"You see what?"

Danny refilled both their glasses, "John."

"I don't get it? Who's John?"

"John was her high school sweetheart. He wrote his name in the dirt on the hood of the passenger side, right where I could see it. Cold, but smart by him." Danny took a long sip. "The first cut is the deepest, Becca."

Her eyes grew wide, "Wow. She didn't deny it?"

He exhaled and didn't let his emotions remember too much. "Nope. They married the following year."

"Damn, you've seen some pain, Danny boy."

"'Bout the same as anyone," Danny added. "I've broken a heart, and I've had mine broken."

"So, does it make you wiser, as they say?"

"Hell yes. Although, I've never really trusted anyone since, to be honest with you. I had a few off and on relationships after that, but nothing serious, besides this latest one. Started going to all my friends' weddings. You'll go through it, too. First, you get wedding invitations in the mail. That lasts a few years. And then you start getting postcards at Christmas with their babies sitting on Santa's lap. And now with Facebook, I recognize my friends' faces in kids I've never met." Danny sat back and wiped his hands on his napkin, "I'm sorry. The wine is making me talk *way* too much."

She smiled, "No, it's fine. Really. You're actually kind of interesting. I knew there would be more to you than just lobsters." she pulled out her phone. "Can I friend you on Facebook?"

Danny laughed, "Sure."

She started typing fast on her phone. Danny admired the speed of her fingers – something that missed his generation. He still employed the 'seek and destroy' method on his keyboard.

"What's your last name?" she asked, not looking up from her phone. Danny looked at her tan shoulders and her dirty blond hair. She was attractive, especially the more you got to know her.

"Bolick."

She typed it in. "There you are," she smiled and seemed to add a note.

Danny pulled his wallet out of his back pocket and put a credit card on the check.

"Nice profile pic," she added.

"Ha. I bet I'm gonna be the oldest friend you have."

"Let me put it this way, Danny boy. I never ask guys out."

"Is that a compliment?"

The waiter came and picked up the credit card.

"You'll have to figure that out yourself," she smiled.

Danny smiled back and they shared another look, "Thank you," he finally spoke.

"For what?"

"I guess you'll have to figure that out for yourself."

She smiled and looked down as she put her phone back into her purse.

The waiter returned with Danny's card, "You folks have a good evening." He added a third smile and left.

"You too, thanks," Danny said. He took the provided pen and added a tip, and then signed the note.

"Shit," Becca quickly said.

"What?" he looked up.

"Should I pay for half? Sorry."

"No, no. Please. You know my secret. It's the least I can do."

"Well, thank you," she said. "Your secret is safe with me."

Danny could tell in her voice that she meant it. They were friends, like they'd known each other for years. He felt a comfort with her. It was a welcome feeling.

She added, "Can I ask you one last thing?"

"Sure," Danny looked to her.

"You didn't really want the fettuccini did you?"

He laughed as they rose from their chairs, "No. But I will order it in the future." He thought that sounded a little too flirtatious. She just smiled. They had just met and they both knew they would see each other again.

Outside a light breeze met them.

"Well, that went pretty well, I'd say," she said.

"Agreed. And the weather only crept in once," they laughed.

"I'm this way," she pointed.

"I'm this way," he pointed in the other direction. "Should I walk you to your car?"

She laughed, "You are so cute when you're nervous."

"I'm not nervous!" he stated like a man.

"I can handle it, Danny boy. And don't worry, I don't drive a RT7."

He didn't correct her, "Alright then. How about I call you in a few days, and we continue this conversation?"

"You do that, Danny boy." she turned and let him watch her walk away.

He did. The more he talked to her, the cuter he realized she was. This could be trouble.

CHAPTER 22

WHEN DANNY GOT home it was about ten pm. He went and sat with his lobsters for a few minutes. Becca was stuck in his head. She was cute, funny, and sixteen years younger than him. He was confused now more than ever.

He pictured bringing a twenty-two-year-old to meet his father and the boys. He decided not to think about it. This had been his first enjoyable day in weeks that didn't involve robbery. That's a good thing he thought and he rose to go in.

Inside, he decided to check out her Facebook page. If only he had this when he was younger. He turned on his computer and while he waited for it to boot up, he went to the fridge for a beer.

He popped open a Corona and threw the cap in the sink. He sat down with anticipation. He wanted to see some pictures of her.

Once online, he signed in and went to his friend request page. There was her face waiting for him. Her profile picture was beautiful. It was her laughing. The picture caught her energy. It was a good choice for a profile picture. He looked at his own. It looked old. He should find a better picture of himself, drinking and laughing at a bar. He was on his boat and looking proud. That's why he used it. She complimented him on it, so he decided to leave it.

He clicked yes to the request, and then clicked on her name to get to her home page. Danny glanced at her wall to see what people said to her. How she interacted with others.

He read a lot of "what are you up to tonight?" or "that was so crazy last night." Unlike his wall, his were older people talk, not where's the party?

Danny tried to think of something clever to write in his status but was coming up blank, so he clicked on her pictures. Lots of party pictures. This was the Facebook page of a girl in her twenties – different albums of different parties.

She had some of her at a beach party. She looked great in a bikini. He felt a little guilty looking at them. Her body was lean and her stomach was flat. Average-size breasts that were perfect for her. She was smoking a cigarette in half the pictures. Danny laughed out loud and pictured her taking him to meet her friends. He clicked on some more of the beach pictures. There she was lying on a beach towel as sexy as—

His computer pinged and a chat window opened. It read, *love The Cubicle!* It was from her. She was online. He quickly clicked off her bikini pictures as if she had just caught him.

He decided to be honest and replied. *I promise I wasn't just looking at pictures of you in a bikini!* He hit enter. It was easy to flirt when no one was around. It made you braver. He waited.

Ping. *Liar.*

Okay, maybe one. Enter.

Ping. *Take me out on The Cubicle some time.*

Damn he thought to himself. Why do I have to sell my boat?

Deal. Enter. *Only if you wear that bikini.* Enter.

Ping. *Are you flirting with me?*

He was a little drunk. *Yes.* Enter. Sorry about *taht.* Enter. *Oops that.* Enter.

Ping. *No apology needed.*

I had fun tonight, Becca. Thanks.

Ping. *I had fun too.*

He waited. *She did too.* He drank some beer and tried to picture her in her room. *Did she have a laptop or tower? PC or MAC?*

Ping. *How about this weather?* He burst out laughing. She was funny. He needed to laugh and she was providing plenty of comic relief. He now realized something that he had known for most of the night. Good or bad, he was going to chase after this girl who was sixteen years his junior.

He typed without thinking. *How about dinner on my boat on Friday?* Enter.

Ping. *Love to, Danny boy.* Ping. *Shall I bring anything?*

Just your jokes, Becca. I could use some more. Enter.

Ping. *Okay. What do you get when you cross a cute guy with some bad love?*

He smiled. Where was she going with this? *I don't know, what?* Enter.

Ping. *A pool full of lobsters.*

Danny laughed out loud again. She was making him laugh at himself. This was healthy. He couldn't wait to see her again.

PING. *Good night Shellfish Saint . . . I get it.*

Thank you, he wrote. *Good night.* Enter.

He signed off and then stood up and walked around the kitchen. Part of him wished she were there now. His ears craved to hear her voice. He needed more of her company. He needed something to do. He needed to stay away from his phone. He smiled – *he needed more lobsters.*

His phone beeped with a new text. It was from Becca. He checked it with a smile.

Actually, I'm meeting a friend for a beer. Wanna join? Or is it past your bedtime?

He looked up in the air. He hadn't gone out for a beer this late in awhile. This was a test. He had to go. He wanted to go. His phone beeped again.

I'll be at The Tavern. Oleander and 2nd. Show or don't show. It's all good.

He smiled and decided not to reply. He would just surprise her. What else did he have to do? He grabbed his keys.

CHAPTER 23

THE TAVERN WAS about a mile away. Danny was there fast – too fast. When he walked in, it was about half-full of loud, drunk college kids. He looked around. She hadn't arrived yet. Why didn't he wait and show up later? He was rusty. He had practically run there to see her. He walked toward the bar for a beer. This was not his place. The music was blaring. It dawned on him that he seemed to be the only person there by himself. Whatever. He bellied up to the bar. Five minutes later, the bartender finally acknowledged him.

"Yeah?"

Danny thought beer or liquor? "I'll have a Corona, please."

"I can't hear you," the bartender snorted.

"CORONA!" he should have stayed at home. He took out his wallet and threw a ten on the bar. The bartender took it and replaced it with a Corona. He put Danny's change back on the bar without even looking at him. Four young and drunk guys came up to the bar.

"Hey Steve, four kamikaze shots," one of them slurred. They were on a first name basis with him.

"You got it," Steve the bartender replied. Steve was a pro. He worked fast with big gestures and poured four perfectly even shots. When he was done, there wasn't a drop left in the snifter. Danny tried not to be impressed.

"Let's do something crazy tonight!" one of them screamed to the others. He had on a t-shirt that was a size too small to show the ladies he had been hitting the weights. He screamed out loud for no particular reason.

"Hell yeah!" one of them replied, bumping into Danny without noticing. Danny just shook his head and took a big swig. This was definitely not his scene.

"Let's go roll Kappa Sigs house!" the muscled dude continued.

"Fuck yeah, those assholes!" another replied. They pinged their shot glasses, took the shot, and then rudely slammed them on the bar.

"No. I've got a better idea," another tight t-shirt belched, "Let's go steal Mofo!"

"Oh, dude. Hell yes!"

"We'll cook his ass and leave the empty shell on their doorstep."

"Yeah!" they all replied. Danny looked over to them in disbelief. *Did they just say shell?*

The one facing him noticed he was looking at them and decided to stare back, "You got a problem, bro?" they all stopped and turned to face him in unison.

It took Danny a moment to realize they were talking to him. "Uh, no. Just wondering what a Mofo is?"

They all started laughing. Danny laughed too and took a drink, "What is it, a chicken?" he pried.

They all burst out laughing.

"Nah, man. Mofo is the biggest fucking lobster you've ever seen."

Danny couldn't believe it.

"That's right," another continued, "too bad that asshole David is the one who caught him."

The biggest of the group added, "Fuck the Kappa Sigs!" They looked back to Danny.

He raised his beer, "Fuck the Kappa Sigs," was all he could say.

"Haha! Yeah!" they all screamed.

"Stevie! Get this man a shot!" Danny smiled and took a sip, "Ah, no this beer is fine with me."

"One shot man!"

The others joined in, "One shot! One shot!"

"Alright," Danny finally conceded. "Let me get you guys a round."

"Fuck Yeah!"

Stevie did his same routine only this time with five shot glasses. Danny pulled out a twenty and set it on the bar.

"That'll be thirty," Steve blankly stared at him.

"Ah," Danny replied as he went to his wallet for more. He pulled a few more out for a tip just to blend in with this asshole. He then stood up and grabbed his shot glass. "To MOFO!" he raised his glass.

"To MOFO!" they all cheered and slammed their drinks.

"You say he's a lobster?" Danny asked.

"Man. Mofo is the biggest mother fucking lobster ever caught. Hence the name Mofo. He's got to be at least twenty pounds."

"I'm getting hungry!" another drunkenly screamed. "Let's eat that bitch!"

The odds seemed to be too big for Danny to just walk away.

"Where is he?"

"Why? You hungry too?" one asked. They all laughed.

"I could eat," Danny said flatly.

"Yeah!" they all screamed. They started chanting, "MOFO, MOFO, MOFO!"

Danny couldn't help but laugh out loud to the absurdity of this coincidence.

"Steve, one more time. Let me buy my boy here another shot." the t-shirt added and he put Danny in a friendly headlock.

"Why not?" Danny added.

"Yeah!" they all chanted. "MOFO, MOFO, MOFO!"

"Where'd they get him?" Danny dug some more.

"They caught him a few weeks ago. That David asshole has a boat."

"David is a Kappa Swig?"

"Sig man! Sigma?" they all laughed again.

Danny smiled, "And you guys are?"

Instantly they all started another chant, "SIGMA PHIIIIII! SIGMA PHIIIIII!"

Steve put the shots in front of them. Danny grabbed his. He was tipsy before the shots, but now he was really feeling it, "Mofo, Sigma Nu, Kappa Sig. I'm either drunk or learning a new language."

They all laughed again, toasted and slammed another. Danny slammed his glass down again! "Let's steal this mother fucker!"

"Yeah!" they all joined in a high five.

Danny kept nudging, "So where is he?"

"At the Sig house in a big-ass fish tank. They've been having week-end parties and showing him off like a trophy for the last two weeks."

"Fuck the Sigs," another added. "I'm tired of hearing about it."

"Yeah, fuck the Sigs," Danny added, trying to be part of the team. "I'll steal that bastard for you."

"Oh, shit. I've got it," one of them added. "Have you guys heard about the guy who's been stealing lobsters and then writing a note? We'll write on the tank. Thanks for dinner, *The Shellfish Saint!*"

"David will be madder than hell," another added. "How in the hell are we going to get him out?"

"There's a basketball game tonight," the big t-shirt stated.

"It's true. We're playing Charleston tonight. They'll all be at the game. The house will be empty right now."

"So, what's the plan?" T-shirt asked. They all thought for a moment. Danny decided to speak up.

"I tell you what. I've got a pick-up. You show me where that house is, I'll pull up to the front door and steal that mother fucker, throw him in the back, and drive away," he couldn't believe what he had just said.

They all seemed to look at him with admiration. He was in. The guy in the tight t-shirt looked at him close and shook his head up and down, "Alright, alright. What are we waiting for?"

"Waiting on you," Danny looked him right back in the eyes.

T-shirt stood up, "Steve, hold my tab. We'll be back in a few. Let's roll!"

"Let's roll!" Danny screamed. It came out a little dorky.

"Making friends I see," Danny heard a sweet familiar voice behind him. He turned to see Becca and two of her friends.

"Oh, hi ladies," Danny slurred.

"Are you drunk?" asked Becca.

"No, no. Just did a shot," Danny lied.

"Let's roll man," one of the guys interrupted.

"Yeah, you coming or not, man?"

"No. No. I'm coming," Danny stood up. "I'm sorry," he said to Becca. "I have to go take care of something. I'll explain later. Hi," he said to her friends.

"Hi," one of them returned coldly.

"Meet you outside," one of them said to Danny as they walked away.

Danny looked to Becca trying to think of what to say, "I'll explain later. You won't believe it."

"That's cool," she let him off the hook.

Danny awkwardly squeezed by them and headed for the door.

He walked outside and wondered what he was doing. He came here to meet Becca, but things had taken a different turn. The alcohol was making it hard for him to focus. He shouldn't even be driving. A car pulled up to him by the front door.

"You still in, bro?"

"Yeah," Danny replied. "I'm parked right over there."

A chant from the back seat started, "MOFO, MOFO."

"Follow us," T-shirt said.

Danny walked to his truck trying to clear his head. He had no idea what he would do if he were even able to grab the lobster. He decided not to think. He got in his truck, took a deep breath and turned it on. As the car pulled up to him he heard loud rap music and the Mofo chant still going from inside.

"Right this way," a voice from the car said.

"Right behind you," Danny replied.

CHAPTER 24

THEY PULLED UP to a large house. A hand from the car in front pointed out the window toward it, and then the car slowly pulled forward and cut off its lights. Danny pulled a little past the house as well and turned off his lights. He left the motor running. As quietly as his old truck would let him, he exited.

He looked into the darkness where the other car was in front of him. He heard some giggling as they tried to keep quiet. Danny turned toward the house and slowly walked through the front yard toward the front door.

As he approached, he crept low and squeezed between some bushes to look into one of the windows. It seemed to be quiet and empty.

"Boo!" Danny jumped as he heard the voice behind him. "Don't worry, it's just me." T-shirt had decided to join him.

"It looks empty," Danny said.

"I bet you the back door is open," t-shirt whispered.

"What makes you say that?" Danny asked.

"Ours always is. Follow me."

Danny followed him to the back door. They looked through two more windows before continuing to the back. As they came to the back door they slowed. T-shirt gave him the shhh finger and slowly tried the door. A big smile came over his face and then he slowly opened the door.

"After you," he said to Danny with a malicious smile.

They entered the house. T-shirt tapped on Danny's shoulder and pointed to a room toward the middle of the house. They snuck toward it. Some lights were on, but they didn't hear any voices.

"In there."

They entered the living room and sure enough a giant fish tank was on the table. Inside was the biggest lobster Danny had ever seen. It truly was a Mofo. Danny realized he was probably looking at a hundred-year-old creature.

T-shirt whispered to Danny, "Mother fucker!"

"Yes. I see," Danny replied.

He moved past Danny and plunged his hands right into the tank and pulled the lobster out with one giant motion.

"Wait," Danny said and they froze, only water dripping from the fleeting legs of this massive creature made a sound. They heard voices coming up the back steps.

"Shit. It's David!" T-shirt shouted, "Front door!"

They ran to the front door as the back door opened. A trail of water followed them. Danny tried the handle as T-shirt struggled with the lobster. It was locked.

"Dead bolt, Einstein," Danny heard from behind him.

"Right, got it." Danny slowly unlocked and opened the door and then shut it behind them. They scurried across the front yard toward their cars. T-shirt proudly paused in front of the truck to show his friends his catch. He put out his tongue and waved the lobster around triumphantly. They heard some loud voices coming from the house. Angry voices.

"Put him in the back of the truck!" Danny whispered loudly. They heard the front door of the house open.

"Fuck," T-shirt ran to the truck and dove in the back with the lobster, "Go, go, go!"

Danny frowned as he jumped in the driver's seat. He hadn't planned on one of them riding with him. He was planning on ditching them once he had the lobster.

The vehicles started and pulled away just as they heard footsteps approaching. They sped away with the gas to the floor. They made a quick right and then after a few blocks turned on their lights. Danny could hear screaming from the car in front of them. He opened the sliding window behind him.

"That was fucking close," shouted T-shirt, laughing.

"I know!" Danny shouted back. "You want to jump up front?"

"Hell yeah. This bastard is scratching the shit out of me."

Danny quickly pulled over. This was his only chance. Just as T-shirt jumped out the back, and his feet hit the ground, Danny mashed the gas and turned hard on the steering wheel.

"You mother fucker!" he heard from behind as he pulled away.

He looked in his rearview and saw the other car's reverse lights come on as it turned backward toward the cursing T-shirt. Then he saw headlights coming in his direction.

Danny made a quick right and kept the gas mashed to the floor – his barking wheels turned the corner. At the next block he mashed the steering wheel and turned on another corner, all the time checking his rear view for lights. He had to be careful. If the cops came after him, he would be done for, but he couldn't slow just yet. If those college kids caught up to him, they would surely whip his ass and Mofo would be done for.

He came around another corner and slowed to the speed limit and then came to a stop light at College Road. It was a busy street. He saw lights approaching in his rear view. He put on his blinker and made a quick right and blended into traffic. He slowly caught his breath the further he got away. Ten minutes later he pulled into his driveway and drove right up to the pool. He turned off the ignition and sighed with relief. Then he broke out laughing. He laughed a good two minutes before getting out of the truck. He continued laughing as he walked around to the back and opened the gate of the truck. There sat Mofo, looking right at him.

He climbed into the back of the truck and lay down looking at her. Her power claw was twice the size of his own hand. He just smiled at her in amazement, "Mofo."

CHAPTER 25

DANNY HAD BEEN staring at his phone for ten minutes, waiting for her reply text. His text simply said, "Can I explain?" Clearly, she was mad. If he could only explain it to her, surely she would understand. He let her down by leaving with a bunch of guys the night before. She should be pissed. He picked up his phone. This fix would take a call.

She let it ring four times before picking up. "Damn right you need to call. You can't get away with just a text, Danny boy."

"I'm sorry," he replied. "Can I explain?"

"I get it; you wanted to join a fraternity, but Sigma Phi? Those guys are jerks."

Danny broke in, "You know those guys?"

"Yeah, Danny boy. You didn't seem like the type to hang out with them."

"I wasn't hanging out with them."

"You seemed to be having fun when I saw you."

Danny paused and took a breath, "Can I explain?"

"You don't need to explain anything to me."

"I do. I don't want you to get the wrong impression of me. Look, Becca. I couldn't wait to see you last night. I never go to bars that late anymore. I only went to see you. I like talking with you."

"I like talking with you too," she said. "So why did you leave the moment I got there? My friend said I should keep clear of you."

131

He jumped in, "I know how it looks. Here's what happened. I practically ran to the bar the moment you asked me to meet you there. I was there way too early, so I went up to the bar and ordered a beer. These guys came up and I overheard them talking about this giant lobster that some other fraternity had."

"Mofo?" she asked.

"You know who Mofo is?" Danny asked back.

"Yes. I went to one of their parties last week."

Danny cleared his throat, "Well, he's in my pool now."

"You stole Mofo?" she laughed.

"Yes. I couldn't believe what I was hearing at the bar. They were going to steal him, to piss them off. So, I made friends with them and said I would steal Mofo for them."

"You are one interesting person, Danny boy."

Danny laughed, "They were going to boil him. I couldn't let that happen. What are the odds? I had to save him."

"Yes. Well, So, I guess you won't be giving me your fraternity ring?"

Danny laughed again, "Uh, no. And if those guys ever find me, I'm dead meat."

"Well, at least you're not at home moping around about her."

Danny spoke up, "Are we still on for this Friday?"

"I guess I can give you another chance," she answered.

"Great," he said happily.

"See you then, then," she chirped.

"See you then, then," he replied.

CHAPTER 26

DANNY ROLLED DOWN the window and took a deep breath. He should probably turn around. Becca was controlling his thoughts. He was far from focused, yet he still headed for the docks. The cool air was breaking into his truck. *The lobsters need you.*

Danny pulled up to the docks where the lobster boats slept at night. He sat in his truck and stared at them for a moment. His father's fishing boat was docked at this marina. He needed his father. If he ever got caught, he knew his dad would never speak to him again. It would shame him. Embarrass him. His son stole from his peers. Intruded on their livelihood. Lobsters don't have feelings. *Bullshit.*

It was after midnight. His father's peers would be here in a few hours. He knew they went out early but he didn't know the exact time.

He pulled out his cell and opened his pictures. The last one he took opened first. It was her, his first lobster. The night she tried to bite his finger off. Of all the amazing appendages that a lobster has, it's the eyes that grab you the most. Black, no pupil, no eye socket, yet a soul inside. He knew it. He sensed it.

Danny took another deep breath. *The Shellfish Saint* was still in him. He turned off the ringer and opened the door.

He put on his blond wig instinctively now and pulled the mask half way down. Two black gloves, the bolt cutters and a bag were all he took.

Danny knew that most of the lobster boats had large coolers by them where the owners kept a light day's catch. He was hoping this had been a slow week. They only sold them when the coolers were stocked enough.

He stepped onto the dock. The wood creaked beneath him, as he walked toward the boats. He was in the open, but no one seemed to be around. The lobster boats were to the left. His father's boat was to the right. He didn't even take a glance. This was not the time to think of Dad.

He crept slowly down the narrow dock – his large claw at the ready. If anyone saw him here he was done. The bolt cutters would alert them to his plans.

He approached six lobster boats. Death was in the air. Its smell alerted his senses. This was the last place many creatures of the sea would ever see the ocean. Not this catch, though. Their savior had arrived.

He approached the first cooler. It was large and just as Danny had remembered. It had only a master lock to keep out intruders.

It was no match as Danny's claw closed in on it. One loud pop from the bolt cutters and he was in. Just before opening the lid he looked around to see if anyone had heard the noise. There was no one there. He opened the cooler and found no one there either.

"Shit," he cursed. There was nothing there but white cooler walls.

He proceeded to the next, and popped off its lock. Again empty. Danny wondered what he should do. This would be the only time he could hit the boats. Their broken locks would lead to better protection next time. And eyes.

What's done is done. I might as well check them all.

The third cooler held what Danny was looking for. Their dark bodies stood out against the white cooler. Danny pulled out five rather small lobsters. A small find, but a find nonetheless. Their claws already bandaged. He lowered them into the bag, and then pulled out his pen and signed the guilty cooler. He proceeded to the next.

He put the claws of the bolt cutter over the lock. Breaking master locks this way proved to be strangely gratifying. It gave him strength and power. He popped the lid open to see his prize. Nothing. He had hoped to get more on this—

The wood from the two-by-four struck him squarely on the side of his right arm. The pop echoed off the pier. Instead of flying off sideways as he should have, he remained strangely attached to the wood.

A voice spoke, "Welcome to the docks, asshole."

The pain was numbing. Danny was still confused about what had just happened. The intruder tugged at the wood. The rusty nail that was sticking through the wood and into Danny's right shoulder ripped through his flesh and the dockworker tried to retrieve it for another swing. The piercing metal inside his skin was the worst pain he had ever felt. He almost blacked out, but then screamed in agony as the nail pulled free.

Danny's shirt filled with blood. He turned to face this intruder, this monster of a man. Danny cupped his left hand over his right arm instinctively to stop the bleeding.

"Doesn't feel too good does it?"

Danny never saw the fist coming that now struck his jaw. This time he did crash into the ground, the bag of lobsters soaring away from him. Danny looked up to see what was coming next. A large man with a large belly breaking through suspenders was leering above him. The Mofo of man. He wore a full beard and long angry hair.

The man took a step back, "You robbing the wrong place, son." He came forward with his boot and caught Danny right in the gut knocking the air clean out of him. He was in trouble. The large man knew how to make it hurt. "Since you got me up, guess I'll go ahead and teach you a lesson."

His stepped back again. Danny knew what was coming. He didn't want to feel that pain again or maybe it was the thought of being caught, but as that foot came for his stomach, Danny rolled over and then lunged toward the dockworker. The man's momentum and large belly kept going forward and Danny helped him continue in that direction. The dockworker went right over the side of the walk ramp and into the water. He cursed Danny all the way down and when his head come up for air he cursed some more – and he cursed loudly.

Danny had one thought on his mind – Run! He scrambled to his feet and grabbed the bag of lobsters. There was no ladder for the dockworker to use to pull himself out of the water and his large belly was keeping him from pulling himself up. "You mother fucker! I'm gonna kill you!"

Danny ran or more like hobbled away as fast as he could. The screams chased him as he ran for the safety of his truck. It was the hardest thirty-yard-run he had ever done. The dockworker was out of sight, but Danny could still hear his threats. Someone else was surely hearing this as well.

His truck must have been terrified as well because it started on the first crank. Danny sped out of the parking lot and didn't turn on his lights until he was half way down the road.

He could hardly hold the steering wheel with his right arm. He was seeing stars and his adrenaline was starting to ease the further he got away. At a stoplight he reached for his phone. He needed help, but no hospital. *Who to call?* He should call Kenny, but Stephanie would demand to know where he was going. It was definitely past Brad's bedtime. *What about her?*

The light turned green and he drove with his left hand.

With his right he sent her a text. He could hardly type as his blood-stained fingers searched for the letters. He wrote. *You up?*

Danny drove for a few minutes with his right hand clutching the phone. It finally buzzed. *Yes old man. At the Brown Bar. Wanna join? There are some more frat boys here?*

The throbbing in his arm was becoming unbearable and his jaw was aching. He hadn't realized it until now but his right side rib cage was hurting too. There had to be a cracked rib. He pulled into his driveway and turned off the truck. He sent her another text. *Help. Just got beat up. 1301 Spring St. Sorry.*

He sat in the truck and tried to catch his breath. His arm was now sticky from the clotting blood drying on it. He was afraid to look. This was bad. Danny had never been in a fight before. *Who has a two-by-four with a nail in it?*

His phone buzzed. *You serious?*

Danny climbed out of the truck and stumbled toward the house. His ribs were pounding in pain. They must be broken.

His back motion light came on, revealing his bloody clothes. Danny looked down at his beaten body. He turned on his camera phone and took a picture of his bloody shirt and sent it to her. *No text needed.*

His phone almost instantly buzzed. *I'll be right there.*

His keys fumbled around as he tried to find the lock. This proved to take awhile. He got the door open. He made it. He took a deep breath and tried to compose himself. He had escaped and was now safe under his own roof. He turned on the kitchen light. Through all the pain his house gave him a strong sense of comfort and then exhaustion. He pulled off the wig. He had forgotten that it was even there and threw it over to the side as he collapsed onto his kitchen floor. He rolled onto his back and closed his eyes against the bright light. Deep breaths took over. He wasn't sure how long he lay there, but a car door jolted him back alert. Relax. It has to be her. She went to the front door and knocked. He texted her, *Around back.*

A minute later she came to the back door that was still open.

"Oh my god, Danny!" she pulled his keys out of the door and then closed it behind her, "Are you okay?"

He laughed as he lay there in a puddle of his own blood, "I'm sorry, it's really not funny. I didn't know who else to call."

"Danny we have to get you to a hospital."

"No," his voice now serious. "Surely, he called the cops. They'll be waiting there."

"Who called the cops? What happened to you?"

"Apparently, the large man at the boat dock didn't take a liking to me stealing his lobsters." Danny's eyes widened and he tried to sit up, "Shit! The lobsters. They're in the truck. I'm sorry . . . can you go get them and put them in the pool?"

"Danny you're covered in blood! The lobsters can—"

"Please there are only a few. They need the water or they'll die. There are some scissors in the drawer next to the fridge. Free their claws and then put them in the pool. Please."

"Danny—"

"Please, Becca."

"Alright." She ran and opened the drawer and grabbed the scissors and then ran to his truck. He listened and he heard a door open. The backlight surely turned on so she would be able to see. She handled lobsters so he knew she wouldn't be afraid to pick them up.

Danny suddenly realized how he must look and that this wasn't the most attractive position to be in; he struggled to get up. It was no use;

he was down for the count. His first lobster came into his thoughts. That first night, it too, had been on this same floor, helpless.

A few minutes later, Becca came back inside, "You okay, Danny?" Her concern was comforting.

"Yes. Thanks. It's worse than it looks," he laughed. "I mean it's not as bad as it looks. Sorry."

"Stop apologizing. Where do you keep your Band-Aids?"

His first thought was, *when was the last time I cleaned the bathroom?* "In the bathroom," he said with hesitation. She left the room and he could hear her rummaging through his medicine cabinet. He finally decided there wasn't anything too bad to see in there and he tried to relax again.

She returned and took over like a seasoned nurse. "Where do you hurt the most? Let's start with that."

Danny pointed to where the most blood was and he hoped it wouldn't scare her, "He hit me with a two-by-four – that had a nail in it."

"Oh my god. Are you serious? Okay, let's see it. Take off your shirt."

Danny hesitated. His belly liked the comfort behind a t-shirt, "This isn't how I pictured undressing in front of you the first time." *Yikes, I'm dead on the floor and still I'm flirting with her.*

"You do know how to get a girl's attention, Danny boy." She assessed the situation, "This shirt is already ruined." She grabbed the scissors back off the counter and knelt beside him. Carefully, she cut his T-shirt off. He wished he had been doing more sit ups.

He couldn't take his eyes off of her. This was all very surreal. He had never really lain down on his kitchen floor and this seemed like a new environment. "Ouch!" he let out a scream.

"Sorry. The blood has dried your shirt to your skin. It needs to come off. You *need* a doctor Danny."

"They'll catch me. Please."

She shook her head and continued to get his shirt off. There was a dark hole in his arm and blood was trickling out, "Whoa, it is deep. I need to clean it up. Can you get up? It will be much easier in your tub. Where do you keep your washcloths?"

"There's a closet outside of the bathroom," he hoped she took the top one. There might be one or two girly magazines revealed if she took the one from the bottom.

"Okay, let's get you up," she circled around him and then helped him sit up first. He saw stars and leaned his weight against her.

She held him, "Take your time."

Slowly, he rolled over onto all fours and then stood up. She was at his side the whole time. Together they walked to the bathroom.

"Remember, I said bathroom not bedroom," she said.

He laughed and then grimaced in pain, "Ahhh, don't make me laugh. I think he cracked one of my ribs."

They reached the bathroom and she turned on the light for him. He looked around to see if anything would embarrass him. It all seemed to be in order. The toilet could use a scrub. He climbed into the tub, and lay back.

Becca went into the hallway where the Playboys were and retrieved some towels, "You're gonna need new towels after this."

"Just take a few then," he said with a nervous tone. He tried to get a better look at the wound. It did look deep and he did need a doctor. He decided not to look again.

She returned and ran the tub water until it warmed up. She then soaked the towel and came next to him. She started wiping blood off his body and worked her way up to the wound. "Man, he really got you good. Can I ask you something?"

"Yes, what?"

"How in the hell did you escape? It looks like he got the best of you. I mean . . . did you *kill* him?"

Danny laughed again, "No. He's fine. He just got a little wet." He touched his ribs to see if they were broken, "After he hit me with the wood, I think he punched me first and then kicked me. I don't really remember. All I do remember is that I saw that giant boot coming at me again and I didn't want any part of it. I dodged his second attempt and his momentum carried him into the water," Danny laughed and grabbed his ribs again in pain.

"What?"

"He had a big belly and couldn't climb out of the water."

"You left him bobbing in the water?"

Again he laughed and the smile faded as he thought about it, "It was almost over tonight. For a moment I thought it was. All in all, I'm really lucky."

"Yeah you look it." she washed the blood off the towel and wet it again. She finished washing the blood off and then opened some gauze and tape, "I'll have to get some better bandages in the morning, but this should work for tonight." She applied the large gauze pad and taped it over him. His teeth ground together as he fought against the pain. His thoughts returned to her beauty. She had a nurturing spirit. The more he looked at her the more he wanted to kiss her.

After taping him up, Becca wet a smaller washcloth and wiped the blood off his face. His lip was split open and she slowly dabbed the cloth on it. Her face was very close to his. *It was actually sexy,* he thought. He wondered if she felt it too. Their eyes met for a moment and they both sat there staring, wondering. She gave him a quick peck on the lips, "All done. Let's get you to bed."

He smiled.

She shook her head, "That didn't come out right."

She went to stand up and he grabbed her arm, "Thank you."

"Don't worry about it. I get those kinds of texts all the time. Those jeans have blood on them. You should leave them in the tub. You got some pajamas or something?"

"Yeah. They're under my pillow."

She went in the bedroom as Danny stood up. She came back in and handed them to him. After an awkward moment she comically turned around and covered her eyes.

Pulling his pants down proved to be almost impossible, and he wished they had been dating for years, so it wouldn't be awkward for her to help. They hadn't, though, and it would be, so he fought back the pain and dressed himself.

"All done," he said sounding like a child.

"Okay, should I make you brush your teeth?"

He laughed and squinted in pain. She grabbed his arm and put it around her as he climbed out of the tub. They walked to the bedroom arm in arm, "Where's the light?"

"By the bed, there's a lamp."

She walked ahead and turned it on and then pulled back his bed sheets. He remembered making the bed this morning and was happy that he had.

He climbed in. It was warm and safe. He was in a good place. His heavy eyes took over. The exhaustion returned and he faded to sleep quickly.

"Good night, Danny boy," he felt a kiss on his forehead or maybe he dreamt it.

CHAPTER 27

DANNY SLEPT MOST of the next day. Periodic bouts of deep snoring woke him up and then he faded back to the comfort of the dream world.

Around four he turned over and noticed the spot next to him had been slept in. *She stayed over.* Had he snored too loudly? Did he have a morning erection when she got out of bed? These were things that were happening too soon in their relationship. They just met and she had already seen him in his pjs. Maybe he was being too old-fashioned. She was in her college years. Strange beds the norm.

Turning on his side brought Danny's attention back to the present. He tried taking a deep breath and stopped half way – bad idea. He heard someone rummaging around in the kitchen. *Wait. She must still be here.*

Slowly, his feet managed to find the floor. He made his way to the bathroom and shut the door. His face wasn't as bad as the rest of his body. A small cut beside his mouth was the only sign of violence.

There was a knock at the door, "You're alive, then?"

Danny smiled to the mirror, "Most of me, yes. I was hoping to take a shower. Not sure if this cut is too deep for it, though."

"Yes. What you need is a hot bath. Open the door and I'll run it for you."

His hair was mostly on one side of his head from the pillow, "Uh, I got it."

"Don't be silly, open the door. I got some pills for you too."

"Pills?"

"Nothing psychedelic. For the infection."

Danny frowned and opened the door. He wished his baseball cap were in the bathroom.

"Damn. You do look in bad shape."

"I hope I didn't snore too loudly."

"Funny," she pushed her way toward the tub, "I was gonna say the same thing." She ran the water, adjusting the temperature.

"I can't remember waking up much during the night. Been a long time since I slept like that."

The mirrors steamed with heat. She walked by him and back to the kitchen. "Come take these. I still have them from my dentist, when I got my wisdom teeth pulled. They help fight the infection."

They walked into the kitchen. "Wow, I almost missed the sun today. I'm a regular old college kid."

"Very impressive. I took a look in your pool too. You've been a busy boy. Do you feed them?"

"Yes. Do you remember those two pounds of shrimp I bought from you?"

"Ah, yes. The day you ran from me. Here take these." she handed him a glass of water and two pills, "I'm gonna run out and get you some better bandages. Can I get you anything?"

"Listen, I don't want to put you out; if you need to be doing something." He popped the pills in his mouth and drank the entire glass of water. Their hands met when she reached to take the glass away. She had beautiful hands. Feminine hands. Neither pulled away, and for a moment they stood in the middle of his kitchen like two kids at a dance.

This time he leaned in first and she quickly followed. It wasn't a long kiss nor was it a short peck, but the passion was there. Right there in his pjs and with his warped hair to one side, Danny started another relationship.

"You're sure I'm not holding you up?"

"Don't be silly, I took the day off. Now go take a bath and I'll bring you back some dinner. And don't get that bandage too wet." *This was nice,* he thought. She really was taking care of him.

"Yes ma'am," he headed for the bathroom. "There should be some money in my wallet on the table."

"No worries."

He heard the door shut. The steam had engulfed the room as Danny turned off the water. The silence was nice. A light drop of water from the faucet jumped into his hot pool. He put his toes in to test. It was hot – too hot – as he stepped in. For a few minutes Danny stood ankle deep in a hot bathtub trying to adjust to the water. He thought of the lobsters again. A shiver racked his body. *Boiling. What a way to go.*

He lowered himself into the water. The cold water broke the silence as he turned it on to fight the heat. This was the first bath he had taken in years and now he knew why. But as he laid back and the cold water got the temperature right, he exhaled. *This is kind of nice.* Turning to one side so as not to get his bandage wet Danny dropped his head under the water. When he surfaced, he lay back in the tub and thought of her.

She was sweet to do this. They got the first kiss out of the way. Her lips were soft. He couldn't wait to kiss her again. He thought of Stacy. He hadn't thought of her much. He was hiding from it, and this new girl was helping. It is happening really fast, but who cares he thought. *I'm having fun.*

After about fifteen minutes, and when he saw his pickled fingers, Danny stood up and let the water trickle off his body. He bent over and pulled the plug from the drain. A thought from his childhood crept in. He remembered being scared of standing in the tub as the water drained. Maybe he was scared he'd be swept down the drain. That eerie feeling returned and he stepped out of the tub away from the drain. *Baths.* The water had a pinkish hue from the remaining blood that washed off him.

After drying off, he put some shaving cream on his face. The muscles in his arm ached as he tried to shave with his right hand. *I need pain pills.*

Danny washed off his shaved face and chased some Excedrin down with water from his cupped hands.

He threw on some jeans and a fresh t-shirt. This kind of twisting ached at his body. He was thirsty. A cold beer sounded good.

Danny grabbed a Corona out of the fridge. There were only three left. Cutting a lime might prove to be too difficult so he drank right out of the bottle. It was approaching five o'clock so he decided to turn on the TV to see if his celebrity status had grown.

His couch chair proved to be just what he needed. He sank down deeply into it and sat in silence a moment before turning on the TV. Things were happening fast with her. She was too young for him. He should stop it now, but he wanted, needed to kiss her again. She seemed to understand this situation he was in.

He held the remote and tried to turn on the TV. His remote was a little stubborn. The on/off button was worn and you really had to push it. Maybe it just needed new batteries but he was already sitting down, again. He pushed hard on the button, again. This proved a problem. His shoulder muscle ached with pain every time he tried to use it.

The TV popped on and he turned to ABC to see the local news. Oprah was still on. Danny had no problem watching Oprah when no one was around to pick on him. She was a saint. The number of lives she affected astounded Danny. He wondered if she would understand his plight to help the lobsters – to save them from an unconscionable death. He had read some articles about lobsters that suggested they don't feel pain due to their different immune system. This made no sense to him. If you do something to a creature that kills it, how could you suggest they don't feel it? It made him again believe he was in the right and reinforced his belief that someone had to help them. The article had also said that keeping live lobsters in a cold refrigerator helped to take away their aggressiveness. *No pain. Yeah right.*

Oprah was doing her final monologue. This episode was on family abuse. Oprah was not scared to deal with the touchy subjects, yet she seemed to approach them with a genuine how-can-I-help attitude. Oprah was a saint.

Danny heard a car door. She's back. Danny muted the TV and listened to her walk around back. She already knew that the front door was never used. She came in with some grocery bags. Danny figured she was just getting take-out, but she was going to cook for him. She kept proving to be amazing.

"How are you feeling?"

"I'm alright."

She walked in the room and sat down on the coach beside his chair, "Just watching Oprah, I see."

Busted. "I'm waiting for the news to start to see if I'm on it."

"Sure you are. It's okay for a man to watch Oprah," she stood up. "I've seen this one, it's a repeat. I'm going to attempt to make you spinach lasagna."

"That sounds great. Anything I can do to help?"

"Nope, I got it."

The jingle of the news came on. It was the same anchors as always. "Toyota is making another recall. Diane will have the weather and *The Shellfish Saint* caught on tape? We'll go out to Robert Stevens who is following the story. Hi, I'm Jessica Lynn."

"And I'm Dan Berns, those stories and more on the Five o'clock News." The news jingle played again.

Danny and Becca sat frozen to what she had just said. *Caught on tape?*

The camera cut back to Jessica, "Tonight, authorities are looking for this man." A picture cut in over her shoulder. It was taken from a video camera and was of bad quality. "Robert has been following this bizarre story of someone who has been stealing live lobsters. Robert it seems there has been a break in the case?"

The camera cut to Robert Stevens who was at the scene down by the boat docks. "That's right Jessica. Tonight we believe this video is of the man they're calling *The Shellfish Saint*. I'm standing here with someone who he stole from who owns one of the boats. What happened sir?" He offered the mic forward.

"Well, I guess I was lying in my bed over there, when I heard this pop by the boats. I'm a light sleeper and got up and looked out my window. I seen this man down there by the coolers. So I grabbed my stick and went down there to see what was going on."

"So you had a confrontation with this man."

"I sure did. When I seen him breaking the locks on the coolers I knew he was aiming to steal from me, so I beat on him with my Billy Stick and got a few punches in as well."

Becca piped in, "I see what you mean about the belly."

Danny was still frozen to the TV wondering if the camera had gotten a good image.

Robert pulled back the mic, "But he managed to get away?"

"Yeah, I feel bad about that. This man has been thieving from good hard working people and I hate I didn't get 'em. We tussled a bit and he managed to throw me off the dock into the water and then he escaped."

Brad burst through the back door, "Turn on the TV! There's a video of . . ." he paused when he saw Becca, "Oh."

"Don't worry. She knows. Brad, Becca. Becca, Brad." They all fell silent as the reporter mentioned the video.

"Tonight, authorities are looking for this man. He appears to be just under six feet tall and has shoulder length dirty blond hair."

"Good call on the wig," Brad whispered.

Robert continued as a video of Danny walking by a camera near the parking lot appeared on the screen. It was black and white and Danny relaxed a little when it never caught his face.

"We're one step closer to catching this criminal Jessica. The man in question may be hurt from wounds suffered from his entanglement with this man. Authorities are checking the local hospitals. It appears it is just one man on a mission, a mission to steal live lobsters. I'm Robert Stevens reporting."

The camera went back to Jessica, "Okay, thanks, Robert. Was he able to get away with any lobsters?"

"What's that? Oh yes. It appears there were only five or so lobsters here, so no major theft, but the local fishermen here are not too happy with this sudden vigilante against them."

"Okay, thanks, Robert. Intriguing story. In other news—"

Danny hit the mute button.

Brad spoke first, "It's over man. We got to get rid of them. They have you on video."

Danny defended himself, "You couldn't even tell it was me."

"What did he mean by you might have sustained some injuries?"

Danny and Becca looked at each other. "That bastard hit me with a two-by-four that had a nail in it!" Danny raised his t-shirt.

Brad gasped, "Holy shit! Dude, this is getting crazy like."

"Agreed," added Becca.

"And too many people are finding out it's you," Brad gave Becca some suspicious eyes. He seemed not too pleased that Becca was in the loop.

"Relax. Becca is the girl that busted me and let me go."

"Oh, well thank you for not turning him in," Brad spoke awkward-ly, his tone protective of Danny.

She gave a little tone back to Brad, "You boys are digging a pretty good hole here and all the evidence is on this property."

Brad threw his hands up in the air, "She knows about the pool!"

"Relax Brad. I called her last night and asked her to come here. She took care of me and bandaged me up. There was a lot of blood. He beat my ass, man," Danny let out a little chuckle.

"Would you like to stay for dinner?" Becca asked, letting him know she was still helping out.

Brad could hardly make eye contact with her and decided to leave. "Uh, no thanks. I've got some stuff to do." He turned to Danny, "Did you feed them today?"

"Not yet."

"Okay, I'll take care of it," he gave another look to Becca – the in-truder.

Danny smiled, "Make sure you feed Mofo."

"Who?"

"Mofo. He's in the grocery cart about waist deep. Don't stick your finger in there."

Brad wished they could have a conversation about it, but he felt awkward around Becca. "Okay, I'll talk to you later." He motioned back to Danny and then turned and left.

"Alright." Danny felt bad. He didn't expect Becca and Brad to butt heads, but the energy in the room clearly suggested differently.

She headed for the kitchen, "Not sure that he was too happy to see me. I think I'm breaking into the boys club."

Danny stood up and followed her into the kitchen, "He means well. I guess he was upset because it was our little secret and now there is another member." *What are you doing?* Danny walked up behind her and quickly turned her around. He looked into her eyes and then kissed her. This time it was a real kiss, a passionate kiss, but gentle, as they figured each other out. They kissed the same. His hands stayed behind her neck. He wanted to grab her breasts, but felt it was too soon for that. So they just kissed. And kissed.

She finally broke free and teasingly pushed him away, "Do you want dinner or not."

"I'm starving."

"Well sit down over there," she laughed. "Far away, so I can concentrate on cooking."

"Alright," he raised his arms in defeat. "Are you sure I can't do anything?" he flirted, "To help?"

"You can grab me a beer, Danny boy."

"I can do that," he opened the fridge and grabbed a Corona.

"There's more in the paper bag if you want to chill them."

She bought me more beer and now is going to cook. Yep, he was in trouble. This girl had his number.

"Let me show you a trick," she came over to the bag and pulled out some orange juice. She filled the rest of the Corona bottle with orange juice. She offered the bottle to Danny, "Try this."

"What?"

"Trust me."

Danny took the Corona with orange juice and took a hesitant sip, thinking it would be terrible. He then took a bigger sip, "Wow. That is delicious."

"Lime juice is okay," she said, "Orange juice is better. Now, can you make me one please, bartender?"

"Yes ma'am. Does this drink have a name?"

"I don't know. They were having them at a beach party this summer."

Danny held it up to the light. The orange clouded the beer and made it look refreshing, "I shall call it a Becca Beer." He fixed her one, and then toasted her, "To Becca Beers!"

She laughed but joined in, "To Becca Beers!"

He sat back down at the kitchen table and for the rest of the evening they shared conversation, spinach lasagna, and some Becca Beer.

CHAPTER 28

TWO DAYS PASSED, and Danny was still feeling the effects of his beat-down. He saw little of Brad and wondered what was going on.

He took his morning coffee outside in hopes that Brad would pay a visit. He admired the pool. The bottom was almost completely covered with lobsters. Live lobsters. He should have kept a count, but there had to be close to a hundred, plus one Mofo.

Sure enough he heard the fence squeak as Brad jumped over it, and walked over to him.

"Hey Brad."

"What's up Danny?"

"Just hanging with the friends," he stared at his growing collection at the bottom of the pool.

"She's not here?" Brad said with a hesitation.

"If you're referring to Becca, no, she's not. She had to work today." He didn't mean that to sound as rude as it came out.

"Whatever. How's the arm?"

"Hurting. It feels like I just got a monstrous flu shot in the arm."

Brad laughed a little and then his face got serious. He had something to say and wasn't sure how to bring it up. "I think it's time to free them. That big ass one can barely move in the grocery cart. I was thinking about doing it tonight."

"*You* were thinking about it?" again Danny's voice sounded rude,

"Don't you think that's gonna be my choice? They're not your lobsters." He felt that Brad was invading on his territory.

"How can you say that!" Brad's voice rose, as he moved toward the pool, "They're not yours either!"

Danny squinted his eyes. Everything was beginning to spiral out of control, "Brad, what's going on?"

Brad let his anger out in a shout, "You're being selfish! You keep telling people. Have you thought about what's going to happen to *our* lobsters when you get caught? They're gonna go back to their rightful owners."

Brad was pissing him off even though he was making sense, "Oh, so I'm *The Selfish Saint* now. This is *my* thing Brad. I'll decide when and what's best for them. If you can't handle that you should think twice about climbing the fence."

Brad stood up; his emotions had gotten the best of him. He took a step back but still argued, "Yeah, well, fuck you when you get caught."

Danny paused to think. There had to be something more than the lobsters that was making Brad so aggressive toward him. It had to be about her, "Is this about Becca?"

Brad's voice was cruelly calm, "You mean that girl you're cradle robbing?"

There was another pause before the explosion of screaming. Danny threw his coffee mug on the concrete and it exploded along with his temper. "Fuck you! You little shit! Maybe you're just mad 'cause you can't get a fucking girlfriend." The gloves were off.

"Girlfriend?" Brad mocked with a sneer, "Is that what you call her? More like stepdaughter. I hope they arrest you for that, too!"

A car door shut and neither of them heard it.

"She's twenty-three, moron! And a whole lot more mature than you're acting."

"You're talking to me about mature? Look in your fucking pool, wise guy. Don't preach to me!"

A voice entered the conversation and Danny could not believe who it was, "What the hell is going on here?"

Danny's father had only been to his place twice in all the years that Danny lived there, once when he moved in, and once to meet Stacy for an awkward dinner of meet the parent. Danny even had Brad over that night to help with the conversation. It hadn't worked.

"Dad?" Danny was both confused and terrified of his father being there. He would flip if he noticed what was at the bottom of his pool, "What are you doing here?"

"Looks like I came by at the right time. What the hell are you two fighting about?" his dad asked, perplexed.

"Nothing, Mr. Bolick," Brad didn't want him looking in the pool either so he started to step away. Danny was grateful that he wasn't selling him out.

"Now you just hold on a minute," Danny's father stepped in front of him. "I demand you tell me why the whole neighborhood can hear you two."

No words would come to Danny. He had no idea what to say to his father. All he could think about were the lobsters at the bottom of his pool.

Brad stepped in to save the day, "It's my fault, Mr. Bolick. I wanted to take *The Cubicle* out for a spin and Danny wouldn't let me."

Danny felt admiration for Brad for trying to help. He also felt guilt for what he had said.

His father's voice lowered as he spoke to Brad, "Well son, you are a bit young to be skippering a boat by yourself."

Brad offered no argument, "Yes, sir."

"But why then were you screaming about the pool?"

Danny and Brad both locked up. His father took two steps forward and saw what was at the bottom. You could hear a pin drop for about twenty seconds until his father spoke again.

"Is that . . . ?" He pointed to the pool, and then to Danny, "Are you . . . ?"

Danny put up his hand, "Now, Dad I can explain."

"You're a damn thief? I raised a thief? Your mother is turning over in her grave right now," his voice was rising for all the neighbors to hear now.

"Dad, it's not what you think. Let me just explain."

"You're stealing from my friends, you little shit. They're gonna lock you up, boy, and throw away the key."

"Dad, if you just . . ."

"Don't you dad me!" he was furious. "And you let this *boy* get involved!" He glared over to Brad who took a step back in fear. Danny looked over to Brad's house to see if his father was spying out the window. He didn't think he saw him.

Danny's father turned his attention to Brad and started yelling, "Now you get the hell out of here and don't you come back or they'll hang you too!"

Danny glanced over to Brad. They were both frozen as if they had just been busted for drinking underage. Danny gave him the nod to go. He was the lucky one. He could escape.

Brad ran. He reached the fence in no time and scaled it in seconds.

His father now turned to him. Danny wanted to leave as well – to get as far away as he could. He had never seen such rage in his father.

"Now you listen to me. You're gonna return every one of those damn lobsters."

Danny was an adult now and suddenly filled with anger. He responded with his own threats, "How dare you tell me what to do! You haven't acted like my father for years and now you think you can come over here and tell me what to do. Well, I got news for you—"

His father's voice was cold, "You watch your tongue boy."

"You get out of here!" he shouted it so loud his throat hurt. He had never spoken to his father like that, and he wasn't done, "And don't you ever come back here!"

His father stood his ground, "How do you think it's gonna look on me when they find out it's my son who has been the one stealing this whole time?"

Danny's arms shook with anger. He could feel his heart beat pulsing through the hole in his arm. He was too mad to scream, and almost thought he wouldn't be able to speak. It came out as almost a whisper. "You?" he said it again. "You!" he looked around in anger. "It always has to be about you. When Mom died, I lost my father as well. You, you, you!"

"Now don't you bring her name—"

Danny's voice overcame his fathers, "This isn't about you! It's about me! Don't you even want to know why I'm fucking doing it?" his body vibrated as he screamed.

"Hell no, I don't want any part of it!" his father tried to fight back, but he had never seen the rage that was now coming out of his son.

Danny whispered in a hellish voice, "You get the hell out of here. Now!"

His father turned to leave. Just as he opened the door to his truck he said, "I'll give you two days and then I'm calling the police."

"NOW!" Danny screamed and pointed the way.

His father started the truck, backed out and left.

Danny turned to go inside and saw Brad's father looking out the window at him.

"Mind your own fucking business!" Danny screamed and turned for his house. *I shouldn't have said that.* He looked to his pool as he walked inside. *Everyone is finding out my secret. The spiral is spinning.*

CHAPTER 29

BECCA'S PHONE CHIMED. It was a text from Danny. *In the mood for a boat ride? I need to get out of here.* She smiled and her fingers sent a text back. *Be right there.*

It was getting dark as Danny hooked the trailer up to the boat. The Chinese take-out had just arrived and Danny set it in the cabin of the boat. He also brought two bottles of red wine and stocked the boats cooler with Corona – and orange juice. He straightened up the cabin, in case he was to have a close encounter.

She pulled up just as he was finishing with the boat. She pulled her car off to the side of his driveway leaving them room to get out.

Becca greeted him with a big smile, "Danny boy, what a pleasant surprise."

He laughed and met her halfway. They both knew they were headed for a kiss. They crashed into each other and their lips met hard. Harder than that first kiss you share with someone. They already had that one. This kiss said, "I've been waiting all day to do this."

Their heads pulled back, "You ready to go?" he flirted with a smile.

"I'm ready," She gazed up into his eyes and gave him another peck on the lips.

He would have taken her right then if they had more privacy, but the open ocean called to them.

"I'm just gonna run in and get some more bandages so I change that one."

"Out on the water?"

"Yes. It will be romantic."

That's all he needed to hear. "Okay," he waited for her. She ran inside and soon returned.

"Should I lock it?"

"Please," he said.

She skipped back to his side, "Ready, Captain."

He walked her to the passenger side of the truck and opened the door for her, "Too old-fashioned if I open the door for you?"

Her hand grabbed him under the jaw, "You are so cute," she gave him a quick kiss. He didn't let on that his jaw still hurt. He wanted to kiss her more. They headed for the ocean.

Becca helped as he backed the boat into the water. She held the line of the boat at the pier as he parked the truck.

The pier squeaked as he ran to her, "All aboard!" he shouted from a distance.

"Aye, aye, Captain."

He helped her aboard and then gave a hard push-off with his foot. *The Cubicle* usually took more than the truck's two cranks to start, but tonight she was showing off. She fired right up and Danny swung her around and put it in drive.

They coasted in the inlet so as not to cause waves on the nearby boat docks. Danny didn't mind. The sun was setting and this slow pace added to the romance.

"There's some Corona in the cooler in the cabin," he shouted over the engines.

"Great," she said as she skipped ahead. She turned to him and shouted, "Orange juice?"

He smiled and saluted her.

She disappeared into the cabin.

Alone, Danny took in the breeze. Knowing you're about to get laid will put a smile on any man's face and he couldn't remember wanting to have sex with a woman more.

Becca reappeared with two orange cloudy beers and handed him one, "Can I have a look up front?"

"Sure," they pinged their bottles together and Becca walked to the bow of the boat. Danny watched her every move and wondered if she had walked up there on purpose. She had on solid light-green colored sundress that was tight in all the right places. Her legs peeked out beneath and her toes wrapped around purple sandals. She had beautiful feet. The more Danny looked at her, the more he wanted her.

Their age difference, his father's anger, and the fact that the cops were looking for him all disappeared with the land. She returned and the remaining rays of the sun kissed the back of her hair. She twisted her head sideways to let the wind catch it and blow it out of her face.

She came to his side and put her arm inside his, "It's so beautiful. You'd be surprised at how few times I've been out on a boat."

"You wanna take the wheel?" he pulled her close to him.

"Hell, yes," she smiled and grabbed the chrome wheel. They were coming out of the inlet and into the open ocean.

He pointed to the colored pilings, "Keep the green ones on your starboard side."

"That's to the right, right?"

"Correct. Port is to the left."

She pointed left, "Port, and then right, starboard. I think I can remember that."

Danny then pointed to the red pilings, "We'll use those to guide us on the way back. Red, Right, Return."

"Shouldn't it be Red, Starboard, Return?" she joked.

Danny had a puzzled look on his face, "I've never thought of that." He looked at the back of her head. Her dirty blond hair blew behind her as she skippered *The Cubicle*. She continued to impress him with her cleverness. He looked behind them. They were far enough out, "Want to see what she can do?"

"Okay," she screamed back. She knew where the throttle was and gave it some gas. *The Cubicle* jumped to life. The hull bounced off the waves and rocked them back and forth. The wind made it very chilly. Danny left her side.

"Don't leave!" she screamed and laughed with the bouncing waves, and hung on to the wheel.

"I'll be right back," he screamed to her, his voice barely audible over *The Cubicle's* engines. The noise changed as he went into the cabin. He opened a small closet, and pulled out two matching jackets. Kenny had them made for him when he started his dive business. They were red with a white round life preserver stitched on the back. Above it in cursive read *The Cubicle*. He thought about Kenny for a moment. Almost everyone he knew right now was mad at him. There was a lot to fix on shore, but that was for another day. He walked back up the three wooden steps of the cabin, back to her.

When he came back into view, he modeled his jacket for her, first the front and then the back. She smiled and clapped. He brought the other jacket to her and before giving it to her he showed her its front pocket. It read Captain. She clapped again. He frowned and showed her the pocket on his jacket. There was nothing there. They both laughed. Danny came back to the dashboard and turned on all the lights of *The Cubicle*.

Becca eased the throttle back and the bumping noise quieted. The wake that was behind them caught up and lifted the back end up and then down. "This is so much fun," she said, "I never want to go back."

He laughed, "You hungry?"

"Starving! Fix my dinner crew man!" she shouted. They both took a long drag from their beers. Under the port seat compartment, Danny pulled out the white containers and handed her some chopsticks.

"Don't we need to drop anchor or something?" she asked.

Danny looked around, "Yeah, this looks like a good spot."

"Well, you go do that. I'll set this up."

"Aye, aye, Captain," he said, and he walked to the bow of the boat. He wondered if she checked him out as he had done her. He unbound the anchor and made sure he was clear of the line. He then gave a mighty toss and threw the anchor to the port side of the boat. He let out a yelp, "Awwwww!" his bruised ribs barked at him. He turned and looked back to her. She gave him a frown. He walked back to her and tried to ignore the pain.

"You poor thing," she said as he sat down. "Let me fix you a plate." she poured some rice out of the container and he opened his chopsticks.

"Another beer?" he asked as he finished his.

"Sure."

He got up and went for two more, "Just throw some of the chow mein and vegetables over my rice," he said as he went for the beer.

When he returned she handed him a plate and together they sat at the back of the boat and took in the view.

"It's so peaceful out here," she said.

He turned to her and smiled, "I was just thinking the same thing."

Their chopsticks grabbed at the food and for the next few minutes they ate in silence slowly rocking with the waves.

"I love Mr. Wu's take-out," she said as she put some chow mein in her mouth.

"I do too. I order from them all the time."

"So, how was your day?" she asked, engaging him.

"Terrible," he answered.

"What happened?" she asked, alerted by the bitterness in his voice.

"Dad came by and saw the lobsters."

She gasped, "I take it he wasn't happy?"

Danny took a big drink of beer and stared at his food, "Made it about him as always. We never can see eye-to-eye on anything."

"I'm sure he's just worried about you."

"Yeah, I guess," he mumbled, angry and confused. "Let's not talk about me. How was your day?"

"Uneventful. Same as every other day, until you texted me." she leaned in and pushed her shoulder against his and smiled as she chewed her food. She didn't mention the lobsters she sold today.

"I'm glad we met," he blurted out. "I needed to meet you."

"Ahh, that's so sweet," she leaned in and gave him a kiss. Then another. They were both hungry and it wasn't the food they wanted.

For a moment they held their plates in their laps and kissed. As it became more passionate they dropped them. Their tongues got reacquainted. She pulled her head back as she had his lower lip between hers. She pulled back on it.

Their eyes opened at the same time and they gazed at each other. "You are so beautiful," he whispered to her.

That must have been the right thing to say because she straddled him and their kisses became almost violent. Their faces danced as she would take the lead then him, turning his face on the right for bit and then she turned her head. The boat bobbed up and down as they proceeded to the next step.

She stood up and took off her jacket. He followed her lead. She pulled the shoulder straps off her and the dress fell to the mahogany deck. He watched her as her arms went to her back and released her bra. There was no pause, no sexual dance, she threw her bra to the side and jumped back onto his lap. Her breast went right in his mouth as she pulled him to her. Her fingers stroked his scalp as they ground their bodies together. All his longing for her was now in his tongue as he explored her flesh.

Her hands found his belt and she ripped it off as their lips returned to each other. He was hard. Hard like when he was a teenager. Her hand went down his pants and she clutched him.

He needed her. He needed her now. He picked her up and they stood on the deck. Their lips still locked. She pulled his shirt up and over his head. *Never mind the pain.*

Danny finished pushing his jeans off as she took off her panties. Their eyes never left each other. They embraced again and danced their way down to the deck. He lay on top of her. The tip of his manhood lightly grazed her entrance as the waves encouraged the motion. He thrust into her. Her head tilted back as she took him in. Slow at first, with the rhythm of the waves.

She rolled him over and got on top of him. She sat up and dug her fingernails into his chest. He opened his eyes and watched her perfect body make love to him, the stars behind her getting clearer with the incoming night.

His hands wrapped around her waist. He needed more. His body had to go faster.

Together they rolled over again and he moved his hips like he hadn't in years. He stretched out on his toes and raised himself up with his arms. The bruised hole in his arm pulsated with his pumping heartbeat. He liked the pain. It made him feel alive. He was having well-needed sex and she was too.

He exploded into her and howled at the open air. They froze together at the same moment and then he collapsed on top of her.

His head lay on her breasts as their heavy breathing out raced the pulsing waves. He remained inside her as their breathing subsided. He pulled out of her and rolled over on his back.

A laugh jumped out of her mouth and then his. Under the stars and completely nude Danny and Becca laughed together as the tension was washed away.

CHAPTER 30

BECCA CAME BY the house the next evening after work. They had sent flirtatious texts all day. Danny was beginning to understand the allure of text massaging.

He had waited for her out by the pool with two Becca beers in hand. The sun was headed down and a warm glow surrounded the pool.

"Hello," she said, as she glided up with a bag in each hand.

"Hello," he said back and they shared the next-day-lovers' smile. She ran her hand across *The Cubicle's* hull as she approached. A memory she would keep.

"I brought some shrimp for them," she showed him one bag. "And some more take-out from Mr. Wu's for us. I'm still craving chow mein."

He thought of the rocking of the boat in the waves, "Ah, a reenactment is in order."

She sat down close beside him and kissed him, "Hi."

"Hi."

She gave him a concerned frown, "How's that bandage? Should I change it?"

"Nah, I took a shower earlier and managed to do it."

She handed him the bag of shrimp and he handed her a cold Corona. "This is nice," she said and leaned back to look at the sky.

Danny opened the bag of shrimp and began throwing pieces into the pool.

She returned her gaze to him, "Can I ask you something? And don't get mad, but I need to know."

Danny paused, "Wow. That is a loaded question. Okay, shoot."

"What about the shrimp?"

Danny laughed, "You mean why do I not save them too?"

"Yes," She sat up straight.

"I've thought about that. Two reasons. One, the shrimp aren't kept alive like the lobsters; stacked in tanks waiting to be boiled."

She thought about it, still not certain, "And two?"

He paused, unsure how to put it. *Will she find this insane?* He looked down, "And two . . . the bond."

Her eyes narrowed trying to understand, "The bond?"

"Yeah. I can't explain it really. Some people bond with whales, so they go out of their way to save them. For me, it's lobsters. Even more so, because no one else seems to care about them. Sadly, their tasty flesh is their downfall." He wondered if Mother Nature had something to do with this, "Does that make sense?"

She nodded, "Kind of, I guess. I just have a different point of view on it. It's a lot of people's livelihood. Good honest people."

Like her family, this directly affects her mother and father. He said his peace anyway. "Two billion dollars' worth."

"What's that?"

"Two billion dollars' worth of lobsters are sold a year."

"Really?" She took another drink, "That is a lot."

"I can show you on the computer. There are some amazing lobster facts."

"Yes, but you talk about them as if they have feelings. I heard they don't feel pain."

Is she trying to start a fight with me? What is she really getting at? "How can they not feel? Did you know they can live to be over one hundred years old? They're bound to learn how to feel something. I mean, a hundred years is a long time. They don't just crawl in pot of boiling water."

She laughed awkwardly, "Okay, here is what I really meant."

Danny took a sip. *Ah, the real point. Here we go.*

"It's just how it all started," she tried to explain. "I mean the circumstances. I'm not making sense here." she paused and tried to figure out how to say it. Danny looked at her in silence.

"It all started out with *her* saying no to you. So, isn't it *her* that you are really wanting to save or rather the *you and her . . . and not the lobsters?*"

Danny laughed and shook his head. She wasn't getting it or was *he* not? He shook his head confused. He had been avoiding every thought of Stacy, and wanted to know as well.

"What?" she said and poked him in the arm.

"You women," he grinned at her.

"What?"

"Trust me. She is out of the picture. She has nothing to do with this. Yes it started with that incident. But I'm well beyond that now. We weren't meant to be. I've been seeing things differently. I could never go back to that." his voice was off-pitch.

"Do you still love her?"

"You are so cute. Are you jealous?" he wanted to change the subject.

"No," she added. "Well, maybe. It's just, if a woman can cause a man to go on a lobster-stealing rampage . . ." They both laughed.

"Lobster-stealing rampage?" Danny teased her.

"Yes. That is a major thing. She must have had a major impact on your life," there was jealousy in her voice, but she really just wanted someone who felt that way about her.

He could see this was affecting her. "I haven't even talked to her. It's over. I swear. I hardly think of her since I started this," his hand referred to the bottom of the pool, but he held a lie inside.

"But that's just it, Danny. Don't you see? The lobsters are just masking the truth."

She was digging up something in him that he wanted left buried, "Can't we just talk about something else? Please. Let's eat," he went for the bags.

"I'm just worried about you is all."

The conversation sped up, "And I appreciate it, really I do."

"I just rather it would be me instead of the lobsters that got your mind off of her."

Danny realized how much their relationship had progressed in the last few days. He needed to be careful. She didn't seem to be okay about all this. Instead of playing it smart, he broke out his shovel to dig deeper. Maybe it was a defensive reaction.

"Can I ask you something, then?"

She opened the white containers, "No, you can't." he laughed.

"Maybe," he hesitated, "this isn't really *all* about me."

She looked at him, "What do you mean?"

"Maybe this is about *him*," the shovel landed deep in the dirt.

She poked at the rice with her chopsticks in silence.

He exhaled. *She does still care about him.* "I'm sorry. I shouldn't have brought that up."

"It's okay," she didn't look up.

He didn't know what to say so he poked at his rice as well.

She broke the silence first, her voice filled with emotion, "It's just, I was finally starting to get over him. And then you came along, and I'm really enjoying your company. I really like you, Danny, but . . ."

"But what?" he asked apprehensively.

"But you're a mess, Danny."

A quick breath exited his nose, "Our defenses are both throwing dirt."

"What do you mean?"

"Nothing. I hear you. It's true. I am a mess. I have no idea where I'm going or what I'm going to do. I've been hiding here in the present. No past, no future."

"I can't have two broken hearts in one summer, Danny." She put down her chopsticks.

He knew it just as she said it. It was going to be over before it really started. He set down his chopsticks as well.

He tried to break the silence with a laugh, "Well, this is not what I had in mind for tonight."

"I'm sorry," her voice was sad.

He looked over to her, "Hey, you have nothing to be sorry for. I should have never let you get involved in this, anyway," he put his arm around her. "Listen, I've only known you for a short while, and maybe that is all I'll ever know of you, but know this, I'll never forget you. You are an amazing person Becca Moore."

"I don't want to leave," her voice broke. She was at a loss for words.

He kissed the top of her head and held her. He guessed it would be for the last time.

CHAPTER 31

DANNY WAS ALREADY inside looking out the window as her head-lights waved goodbye. A little shell-shocked. *Another relationship over?*

Maybe she was right. *I am a mess. Is this really all about Stacy? It can't be.*

He woke his computer up. Again, he googled lobster. Purple high-lights in the titles showed pages he had already searched. He scrolled down. None of this was what he was looking for. He knew about them, life expectancy, where they live, their habits. He was searching for something else.

It dawned on him that it was not the lobsters he wanted to search for but the culprits responsible for capturing them. That's whom he wanted to read about.

This time he googled, buy live lobsters North Carolina. He exhaled and then hit enter. He clicked on the first page. Jackpot. This was what he was looking for. The header had two postings on it. The first said order by ten a.m. for next day delivery. The next said overnight ship-ping for only $29.99.

Danny sat back and thought about this. *They box them up and ship them out?* He returned to the computer and read on.

This place did it all themselves. They caught them with their own boat, with their own traps and stacked them in their own tanks, and then packaged them in their own boxes. He squinted at the screen and read on. Next, it talked about sizes of lobsters and their different colors.

He then came to a section called, *"Getting to Know Your Lobster."* This infuriated Danny. Like you were going to read about how to take care of your pet.

He read more. *"Why do lobsters turn red when they are cooked? The other pigments are masked."* The murder was right there and the nonchalant way it was written was offensive to him.

He read on. *"How can you tell a lobster is alive after taking it out of the box? Some may appear weak or lifeless upon arrival. The best way to know is to boil the lobster. If the tail curls when it is boiled, then the lobster was alive when it was cooked."* He read it again. *If the tail curls when it is boiled, then the lobster was alive when it was cooked.* Shivers went down his spine.

The last section awoke the Shellfish Saint. *"What is the red clump of tiny balls in the lobsters tail? You are the proud owner of a female lobster with immature eggs she hasn't released yet."*

Danny grabbed his keys that were beside his computer and stuck them in his pocket.

He then scrolled up to the top of page and copied the name of the place. He returned to the Google search engine and pasted it in the search bar and then added the word *"address."* Enter. 2561 Ocean Drive, Sunset Beach.

He copied the address and then went to mapquest.com and pasted it in their window and clicked *"driving directions."*

The map revealed the route he needed to take. It was an hour and fifteen-minute drive south. He hit print.

He would wait two hours and then pay them a visit, arriving after midnight.

CHAPTER 32

A LIGHT RAIN accompanied Danny on his trip south. Shortly after midnight he pulled into the driveway of Captain Jack's. They're stealing from Hollywood as well, he thought. The building appeared to be a long row of warehouses connected to each other. It was right on the water for convenience. *They are the thieves. Robbing the ocean.*

There were cameras on the back alley so Danny put it in park and jumped out. He rummaged through the bag in the back of the truck and pulled out some duct tape. He then ran around to the back of the truck and covered his license plate. He was becoming quite the crook, and sure looked the part now that he was wearing his eye patch and wig.

Captain Jack's was about halfway down. If you hadn't googled it, you would have no idea what the place was. Just a modest sign told of the building contents. This would be a "get in and get out" escape.

Danny first drove around front. The door was modest enough and even made out of glass. But glass was loud and he had no idea if anyone was around or even inside, so he decided to drive around back. There didn't appear to be any cars there. He turned off his lights. The back was dark just like all the other places. There were no windows in sight, just small, regular doors to each stores back exit.

He didn't want to bust down another door. The sledgehammer proved it could break in, but it was loud, and last time Becca heard him. *Becca.*

He thought of her. Just last night, he made love to her under the stars out in the open ocean. He now decided that was the best sex he had ever had, and smiled.

No time to think about her now. He had to keep his wits about him. There were lobsters inside that needed him.

He saw his opening. Captain Jack's truck was parked in the back. Just above it seemed to be a large air conditioning vent. If he could reach it from the top of the truck, he would make his entrance there. He had a small stool ladder in the back. The truck was also at their loading dock entrance. It seemed easy enough.

He crept up slowly in his truck. His gears groaned as he put it in reverse. Oops. He took a deep breath and proceeded. He put it in park, turned the key back and all was silent.

Quietly, he exited and went for his bag. The sledgehammer and bolt cutter would be too heavy. He put his drill in the bag and checked to make sure his Phillips and flat-headed screwdrivers were there. He threw the backpack over his shoulder and pulled the straps tight.

His truck squeaked as he climbed into the back of the cab and onto the roof. From there he stepped over the hood of the other truck and walked up along the side in hopes that the metal would not pop and dent loudly.

The large windshield of the delivery truck proved to be a little slippery, but Danny managed to pull himself up to the top of the cab.

The back of the truck was higher than he thought. Danny pulled off his bag and swung it up on top off the truck. The next step would take some skill. He would have to jump up to the back of the truck and pull himself up.

Without hesitating he jumped to the back. His fingers caught the edge, and he hung there, in trouble. He tried to pull himself up, but his lack of grip and his age kept him from doing so. He thought of his youth. As a teenager he would have scaled this truck in just a few seconds. Danny didn't like the thought of having to say *"at my age."*

He dropped back down but refused defeat. The side of the cabin had a metal guardrail sticking out that might be used as a step, and the top edge of the cabin on the side seemed to have raised metal that he could wrap his fingers around to get a grip.

Danny paused and looked around. There didn't appear to be anyone in sight.

Again, he lunged for the back with his right leg. His foot got a good grip and he pushed up with all his might and found something to grasp. He had a decent grip, but he should have used his left first. He was facing the wrong way. Awkwardly, his legs found air and he twisted his body to face the other direction. He hands were now twisting and hurting. He dropped down again.

"OhhhKayyy," he said aloud sarcastically, starting to get frustrated. "One more time."

This time he lunged with his left leg, found the step, pushed up, grabbed the grip, and heaved. His right leg found another step and he heaved again. With all his might Danny had reached the top of the truck. A sweat bead trickled down his face. He needed a break.

He lay on the back of the truck and took a deep breath. His ribs reminded him that they might be broken. He looked up at the stars. *"Get up,"* he said aloud, and laughed as he turned over because it reminded him of Trinity in *The Matrix,* forcing herself to get up. It worked.

Danny rose to his feet and looked around – still no one. He proceeded to the window.

Damn. I forgot the stepladder. He walked under the large metal opening. There was no way he was going to reach it without the stool. He laughed to himself again.

He turned around and surveyed the scene. The thought of retracing his steps was not appealing, but he had no choice. *If you're going to do it, do it.* So he reversed his tracks and headed back down to the truck, louder, but quicker. Metal giving in with each step.

Back on ground he found his stepladder in the back. It was a wooden, collapsible ladder with three steps. His arm fit between the steps enough to where he thought both arms could be free to climb.

Again, he took the same route. Using his right leg first at the last stage. He had learned from his mistakes.

A few minutes later he was back on top of the truck. This time a little more out of breath. A smooth sailing heist, this was not.

He opened the stool and stood up on it. There was just a metal vent screen keeping him out. The top screws would be the hardest, but he figured he'd manage. There appeared to be eight screws holding the screen in place.

Danny started with the Phillips head, but the screws turned out to be larger and tighter than he thought. His arm quickly tired. He grabbed the drill out of his back and gave it a few test spins. He admired its strength.

The screws were no match for the drill. He worked the drill slowly so the motor wouldn't be too loud.

By the sixth screw, sweat began to trickle down the side of his face. This job was proving to be a tough one and he wasn't even inside yet.

Danny worried the entire metal screen might crash down, but by the eighth screw it hadn't even budged. It must also be hanging on a lip, his first break of the night. With all the screws removed, Danny stood there for a moment with his arms out waiting to catch the screen. It never fell.

He went back to his bag and retrieved the flat head. He began prying the screen out from the bottom, and just as he thought, there was a thin lip all the way around.

It was heavy, but as the last of the screen pulled free, Danny managed to lay it on the top of the truck without making a sound.

He adjusted the stool and then peered into the hole. He could see light about fifteen yards ahead and figured it was just one more screen till he had access.

Again, he put his supplies in the bag, threw it over his shoulder, and pulled on the straps. It would be a tight fit.

Danny pulled himself up and into the vented shaft. He began to crawl with his lower arms up to his face. His bruises ached but didn't slow his determination. His main worry was the aluminum metal tube stretched and popped from his slightly overweight body. He continued.

As the light came up to him, he peered through the hole. He was high up – too high. There was another truck parked inside, but it wasn't under the vent. There were large tanks to the right of the open room that hummed loud with their ventilation. That was his destination. The lights of the entire place were on, but Danny didn't see anyone. *Must just be to scare away intruders.*

Danny noticed the screws next. They were screwed in from the other side. *Of course.*

He had some thick rope back in the truck. *Way back at the truck.* He decided if he could get the screen off, then he would go back and get the rope.

The bag on his shoulders proved to be hard to remove in this tight space. He felt like a lobster. He, too, had trouble reaching that area of his back. What he did have were fingers and he managed to get the backpack off. It was dark so he rummaged through it blindly. He found what he was looking for and pulled out a pair of pliers – His small claw.

He grabbed a screw and visually with his fingers drew righty-tighty-lefty-loosey. Since he was on the other side, it would be the opposite. *I think*.

He tightened around the screw and twisted it to the right. The great thing about aluminum was that it was a weak metal. His claw over-powered it, and the screw began to back out. He stopped short of loosening it all the way and did the same with the three remaining screws.

Danny then amazed himself when he undid his belt and stuck the buckle end between two of the strips of metal of the vented screen. Once it was all the way through, he pulled the buckle back tight and it turned on the other side of the screen to prevent it from pulling back through.

He unscrewed the rest of the screws until the screen fell free. His belt held it firmly in the air as he held firmly onto it with his hand. He turned the screen at an angle and pulled it inside the shaft with him.

Now for the rope. He figured it would take fifteen more minutes to go back and retrieve the rope. He began to back up.

Twenty minutes later Danny was back on top of the truck, rope in hand sweat on face. He secured the rope around a metal post that was attached to the building using a sailor's hitch. Men of the sea knew their knots.

Danny threw the rope into the vent and climbed into the hole. His body was getting worn out. He hadn't had this kind of work-out in years.

With the rope in one hand he edged his way back to the opening where he paused and gathered his breath. He had been at this for over an hour, too long.

He peered through the hole, again. He figured he was about twenty-five feet up. He searched again for any movement and signs of life. The air-radiating bubbles seemed to suggest the only thing alive in the room were the lobsters.

He grabbed his bag in case he needed any tools and tied it to the end of the rope. He began to lower it inside the building. It didn't reach the ground. *Close enough.*

Danny laughed out loud as he realized what he forgot next. Back in his glove compartment nestled neatly away were his leather gloves. Friction on rope burns the hands. He knew this from working with his anchor lines. He felt the rope. It was softer than his other ropes and didn't have sharp hairs sticking out. *There's no way I can go back again.*

He laughed again when he realized there wasn't enough room to turn around in the vent. He would back out and then back in. His pride in his thievery skills was fading fast. Slowly, he backed up.

Once out Danny pulled himself up higher than the vent and then put his feet in first. He was hot, mentally and physically. He thought about his bed, his soft bed and pillows. *Soon.*

He had finally made it to where he had been aiming to be. He was ready to lower himself into the room and save some lobsters. His feet found the hole as he started backing through it. He got a grip on the rope, and it tugged tight as his weight began to pull on it.

His lower half was through and his upper half was pressing his ribs into the metal. His face squinted as he tried to bear the pain. He pushed through the hole. He was hanging by the rope, thirty feet in the air.

Slowly, he started to lower himself down. His arms were not as strong as he thought. The rope began to slide through his hands. He was losing his grip. He felt the burn. Faster, he put one hand under the other, trying to lower himself. The rope barked inside the vent above as he pulled against it. He wasn't going to make it. His hands began to slide against the rope, and his body began to spin. He grabbed the rope hard and looked around.

He saw movement. Inside a room near the front of the building, Danny saw a man in security blue clothes through a large window. He heard the TV on. Cheers from a game.

A burst of energy filled him. Again he began to lower himself hand under hand. Slipping more with every release. Danny felt his flesh start to remove as the rope slipped between his hands. He almost screamed in pain. He couldn't hold on. It was no use. He let go.

The fall was only about fifteen feet, but Danny fell at an angle. He landed sideways with most of his weight landing on his right leg, compacting into his right ankle that rolled when it met the concrete. The pain was too much.

Danny saw stars. The bright fluorescent lights above him seemed to get brighter. It took him a moment to realize the crash had knocked the breath out of him. But when he went to gasp for air, it wasn't there.

A pain grew in him. It was centralized and grew with each found breath. His brain located the source in his ankle. He wished he would pass out. He rolled on the floor in agony. If he could have screamed, he would have, but his breathing was short and quiet.

A scream jolted him, but it wasn't his. It was a happy scream; a someone-scored-a-touchdown scream. It came from the front of the building. *Did the guard not hear the fall?* The Shellfish Saint was lying on the floor helpless, waiting for anyone to notice and capture him and bind his claws.

His thoughts pushed out the pain. His adrenaline was going full bore. *Sit up, Danny.*

He had rolled his ankle before. Once playing basketball and once while walking drunk on ice. Tomorrow, wherever he would be, there would be a purple swollen ankle with him. It was too soon to tell if it was broken.

His breaths returned and Danny fought to sit up. He started to get his bearings, and dragged himself to his bag.

Maybe it was too many *Rambo* or *MacGyver* episodes as a kid, but Danny pulled out the duct tape with a plan.

He taped and then taped some more around his ankle and over his shoe with tight circles. Over and over until he looked like he was wearing a ski boot. The throbbing felt as if it was going to rip through the tape. He then rolled on all fours and slowly the Shellfish Saint rose again. *Get lobsters. Get out.*

Danny shuffled his way to the tanks like a recently born zombie. Two giant-sized white tanks held the biggest catch he had ever seen. There had to be near a hundred lobsters here. No wonder there was a guard on duty. The loud ventilation units pumping in oxygen to keep them alive were an ally. There were plenty of packaging boxes, but how would he transport them to his truck? He searched for something with wheels.

At the end of the packaging table he saw a cart. It wasn't big but it had four wheels. He hobbled over to it and brought it back to the tanks.

One by one, Danny loaded large shipping containers with lobsters. He stacked them on top of each other on the metal cart. The water was cold and numbed his arms. It had been a long day, and he needed it to be over.

After all dark shadows at the bottom of the tank had been taken, Danny had four containers packed with lobsters. *They must be as miserable as I am.*

The cart proved to be a nice crutch as he leaned his weight on it and headed for the back door, but it was top heavy and he had to move slowly.

There was no back door only a large garage door for the truck to fit through. It would be too loud. Surely the guard would hear it and there was bound to be an alarm.

Danny left the boxed lobsters there and went to see about the guard. He had no idea what he was going to do. He thought about putting a chair under the door now, but what if the door swung inward? As he approached, the game got louder. At least he had that on his side. The room was large and narrow with two doors about twenty feet apart. He crept up to the first door. *Damn.* It opened inward.

Danny got an idea. Maybe it was from a movie or an old TV show. He remembered seeing some yellow, quarter-inch rope by the packaging table. He slid back to retrieve it.

He again approached the first door. It opened inward, and that was a good thing. The door was shut and Danny quickly tied a sailor's knot around the doorknob.

His blood started pumping as he held the rope tight and headed for the second door. The guard's back was to him as he walked along the completely glassed-in room. He was ten feet from the other door and he took a deep breath. There would be only one chance at this. He pulled on the robe to double check his knot. It was tight. He peered into the room. There were several monitors on beside the loud TV. *Shit. Monitors.*

The guard and Danny both noticed it at the same time. Danny was on one of the monitors. He looked back to the center of the room where his wig lay. He hadn't even noticed it fly off from the fall, but the TV had a full picture of him. The camera was right above the door.

The guard let out a startled scream. Danny moved to the second door as fast as he could as the guard rose angrily from his chair.

"Hey! This is a restricted area!" The guard ran for the door as well. It was open halfway. Not even noticing the pain, Danny ran for it at full speed; the guard running as well and going for his walkie-talkie.

Danny reached the door first and pulled it shut just as the guard went to grab it.

"You stop right there!" The guard started to pull on the door. Danny pulled the rope tight and feverishly wrapped it around and around the doorknob. The guard pulled on the door, but it wouldn't open. Danny's plan had worked. The rope stretched but held its ground.

"Sorry!" Danny apologized, not sure why he said it, but turned and ran in the other direction. The guard ran with him apparently headed for the other door. He was screaming the whole time, but Danny didn't hear a word. They reached the door at the same time. Danny kept running and the guard pulled on that door with the same result.

The back of the building seemed like an eternity away. Almost there and a deafening alarm went off. The guard must have pushed a button. He probably had five minutes tops to get out.

To the right of the garage door Danny hit the open button. It barked and rose slowly – too slowly for a thief.

Danny readied the cart as he waited for it to rise. Once high enough, he limped outside to his truck that was waiting right there.

He threw the boxes in the back of the cab without thinking about stacking. He needed to leave and he needed to leave now. He ran around the cab and jumped in. One crank and nothing. Two cranks and the engine roared to life. Drive. Gas. Go. He was out of there.

He had left his rope, his backpack and worst of all, he had left his image on the cameras. If they were recording, the Shellfish Saint was out of luck.

He sped onto the road. As the sounds of the alarms subsided, he headed north on Ocean Parkway. Safe – for now.

CHAPTER 33

DANNY'S ANKLE WOKE him up later the next day. By the time he had unloaded the lobsters and freed their claws it was five a.m. He had fallen into a deep sleep shortly after.

His first thoughts this morning were of his face caught on the security monitor. He tried to accept the fact that this could be the end. This might be the last time he would sleep in this bed for a while. He took advantage of that and returned under the covers.

He was still in his same clothes. The ankle still wrapped in its duct tape boot. As bad as things went last night, he impressed himself with his adaptation to the situation.

The rope. He wondered how long the guard was locked in that room. What stories he was telling? How good of a look did he get, and most of all had the record button been on?

He tried to forget about everything. His head hurt from sleeping all day, something he was not used to doing. His dramatic change in lifestyle was not getting along with him.

Inside the *Bay Nine News* station sat Robert Starnes. His desk was clean for a journalist. He had gone digital. Notes were kept on his smart phone or written on his computer.

A small monitor on Robert's desk shouted to him, "Mr. Starnes. Call for you on line two."

He picked up the receiver and sat back in his chair, "This is Robert."

"Let me guess. You're leaning back and got your feet propped up on the table?"

Robert laughed and sat up a little more straight, "Chuck, you devil." Chuck had been Robert's college roommate. The two of them had majored in journalism; Chuck taking the written word route and going to work for a newspaper, and Robert the more glamorous TV journalism. If they were in Hollywood, Chuck would be a writer and Robert the actor.

Chuck's desk was completely different than Robert's. He was surrounded by paper, on his desk, on the floor. The same went for all his colleagues and their desks. Repetition was part of daily journalism and the newspaper industry was doing its best to fight the digital age.

Chuck had taken a smaller job with a smaller paycheck two hours south at the Sunset Times.

"How the hell are ya?" Robert asked his friend, whom he hadn't talked to in awhile.

"Same as always, Robert. Linda had her baby."

"Ohh, congrats. That makes three, right? You better slow down, old man."

"I hear you, friend. I forgot about the joy of not sleeping, but that's not why I'm calling."

"Oh."

"Go check your fax machine, and call me back."

"Fax machine?" Robert said almost sounding offended. Even Chuck's means of communication were old school, a nostalgia he used to love to argue about over a beer with Robert.

"That number still works right?"

"Hell if I know," Robert taunted.

"Well if it does, then I just saved your ass again. Call me back," he hung up.

Robert sat there a moment, intrigued.

Chuck was a good reporter and the two of them made quite the team in college, Yin to Yang. Robert laughed at the thought of Chuck not sending the photo in an email. He was old school. Using the fax machine instead. Newspaper reporters liked paper and weren't giving up on it just yet.

Bay Nine News was a fairly large building. Robert walked to the other end of the building to where he believed the fax machine to be.

Sure enough, sitting by itself on the tray was a sole piece of paper. The journalist in him was excited. Chuck wouldn't send him a fax unless it was something really good.

He picked up the paper and turned it over. The other side revealed a picture of a man caught on a security camera. Written below it with a pen read, *You owe me!*

His intuition kicked in. A smile wiped across his face. He knew who this man was staring back at him. The paper felt good in his hands. He also knew Chuck would argue that point to him later, that seeing it on a computer screen just wasn't the same.

Robert hurried back to his desk, to Chuck, his savior. He grabbed his cell, went to his contacts and tapped on Chuck's name. Another peeve of Chuck's. He'd rather memorize someone's number. It was more personal.

"Chuck here."

Robert could hardly contain himself, "Okay, you've got my attention. Who is it?"

"Seems like your little lobster bandit paid my town a visit last night."

Robert pumped his fist in the air. This was a journalist's best moment when on a story. Getting a picture of the person in question. Putting a face to the story made it more intriguing, more personal.

He was already snapping to his secretary to go get his producer. This was going to be the lead story on the five o'clock news.

"Chuck, you're the best. Kiss the wife and kids."

"Go get 'em tiger."

Robert hung up his cell and stared into the man's eyes in the picture, "Got you."

CHAPTER 34

DANNY DIDN'T KNOW what to do with himself. His bed was too comfortable. He pondered just going back to sleep, but the pain in his ankle was too much. He needed some Excedrin, but that involved getting up. He took in a big yawn and his ribs reminded him of their situation. He was beaten and broken. *Time for a vacation.* Only problem was he had no one to go on the vacation with.

He heard a car door shut. Lately, that was a noise he didn't like hearing because it could be someone with handcuffs. He sat and waited. He waited some more. There was no knock at the door. His heart beat a little faster. *I know I heard a car door.*

Two minutes past and he knew he had to get up. This was too weird. He kicked off the sheets, and took a deep breath. Slowly, he moved his right leg to the floor and then his left. He smelled his under arms, just as he suspected, he was due for a long, hot shower.

He rose and decided that at least a change of shirt was in order. He threw the old one onto the floor of the closet and put on a black one.

He walked to the kitchen to get a look at what car was there. He crept slowly. One, because he was hurt; and two, because his little voice told him to.

Danny froze as he looked and saw the silver Volvo sitting in his garage. *Stacy.*

For a moment he wished it had been the cops. What did she want? And more importantly where was she?

He walked to the back door and sure enough there she was standing over the pool, frozen. *She created this*, was all he could think.

His bed called to him. It was soft. He wasn't ready for this. What would he say to her? Instead, he grabbed a water out of the fridge and went to get it over with.

The squeak of the door didn't snap her out of her trance. *This is bad.* Danny looked down to his taped foot and then felt his unshaven face. He looked a mess. *This is really bad.*

Not knowing what to say he just walked up to her and stood there in silence. He didn't really have anything to say, so if she wanted to talk, she would need to speak first. She did.

"I knew it was you," she said plainly. Not looking at him and barely audible, "I knew the night I saw it on the news the first time. I just didn't want to admit it. This is terrible. I feel like it is my fault. Danny, they're going to put you in jail. Look at all these lobsters." She finally looked at him, "Why are you doing this?"

"You wouldn't understand," Danny whispered. He was tired and didn't know how to explain this, "It's so much more than that now."

She hesitated, "More than what?" her voice cracked.

He didn't answer. She wouldn't understand. What was the use in trying to explain? His father didn't get it. His best friend didn't get it. Stacy would definitely not get it.

"Say something," she grabbed his arm, and for the first time really got a look at him. She looked down and saw his foot, "Danny, my god! What happened to you?"

"It's nothing. I'll be okay."

This was all too much for her. Her emotions got the best of her. She screamed really loud, "NO, IT'S NOT GOING TO BE OKAY!"

They both went silent. As Danny thought about it, he started to get mad. *Who the hell does she think she was? She has no say in this. She had her chance and she said no. I don't need her approval!*

"Say something, Danny!" she barked.

"Like what?" his voice was as loud as hers. "What the hell do you want from me?" he lost it. "Why are you here? You don't get a say in my life *now*. You opted out, remember?"

"Danny, I still care," frustration was in her voice now.

"Bullshit! All you care about is yourself and what all this means to you. Well I got news for you Stacy, I'm over it! I've got nothing to say to you!" He stomped off as best as the duct tape would allow him to. His bed didn't sound like such a bad idea after all. This was all a little too much. He didn't expect to lose it like that, but he also didn't expect that car door to be hers. There was nowhere to hide. He heard her footsteps following him.

CHAPTER 35

ROBERT STARNES HAD the entire staff at his disposal. They had a face. Now, they needed a name. He would go live at five. He needed a name.

All the phones were abuzz. People were moving faster than a regular day. They had many calls about the Shellfish Saint. People claiming to be him or saying they knew who he was. It was always like this, when there was a big story. People wanted to be on TV. Robert didn't really blame them. He wanted to be on TV as well. He understood the allure of it. However, he needed facts. He needed that damn name.

Everyone was now making follow-up calls on the leads. Someone might recognize this picture.

"Elizabeth, where are you with those numbers?" Robert was getting frustrated. It was already four thirty.

"Here you go, Mr. Starnes," Elizabeth came in with a stack of papers – too many papers.

"No. It's not those. It was right here yesterday. There was a guy from a restaurant with a lobster story. Get me that number."

"Yes, Mr. Starnes." She left to get more paper. Robert sat down and picked up the picture again. *Who are you?*

His office phone rang. He quickly picked up the receiver, "Robert here."

"Mr. Wilson on the line for you," his assistant said.

He cupped his hand over the phone, "Shit." Steve Wilson was the boss, "Okay, put him through."

He heard his boss clear his throat and then, "Talk to me, Robert. Tell me you got something."

"I'm working on it, Steve. We are getting close."

"CNN is going to put you on if you can break it, Robert." did he just hear what he thought he heard? "Tell me you can break it, Robert. They aren't going to put you on with just a picture."

"I'm on it, Steve. I just—"

"Found it!" Elizabeth burst into the room.

"I need to call you back, Steve."

"Get me that story!"

Robert hung up. An excited Elizabeth thrust the paper to him, "It's *The Fisherman's Shack* on the pier. The maître d's name is Paulo."

"Yes. That's the one." he grabbed the paper and went back to his phone. This call had come in a few days ago, something about a wedding proposal with lobsters. He was going to go with it anyway, because people loved to hear the story when the girl says no. His journalistic intuition also told him to make the call. He dialed the number and checked his watch. This is why he got into journalism.

"This is The Shack; can you hold, please," a squeaky voice said as she snapped her bubble gum.

Without waiting for an answer, Robert Starnes, who was "on at five," was put on hold. His pen tapped on the desk.

After what seemed like ages the voice returned, "Pick up or delivery?"

"Uh, no," he stood up, anxious. "Is Paulo working tonight?" his face squinted as he leaned back and prayed to the heavens that he was there.

"May I ask who's calling, please?"

He danced in place and pumped his fist. Then he gathered himself and gave his on-air voice. "Can you please tell him that it's Robert Starnes from Bay Nine News returning his call." *Please know who I am, please know who I am.*

There was a pause, "You mean the guy on TV?"

He fist pumped the air again, "Yes, I'm the guy on the TV."

"Is this is that reporter, Robert, who does the news?" she sounded excited. He sensed she sat up and straightened her hair.

"Yes. And I'm on a bit of a deadline here. Is Paolo in?"

"Is this the story about Mr. Lobster? That's what we call that poor man. What a way to hear no."

Robert was getting frustrated but had to be careful what he said, "Yes, dear, and like I said, I am in a bit of a hurry."

"PAULO!" she screamed in his ear. "A Mister Robert Starnes from Bay Nine News is on the phone for you," she continued in a rush, "He says it's urgent. He's coming, Mr. Starnes. He swears that Mr. Lobster is the Shellfish Saint himself. Is that what you think?"

"Well, dear, that's what I'm here to find out."

"Bye, mister reporter," she popped her gum, giggled, and gave the phone to Paulo.

"This is Paulo Squitti," a voice said proudly with a strong Italian accent.

"Mr. Squitti, My name—"

"Please, call me Paulo."

"Okay, Paulo. My name is Robert Starnes of Bay Nine News. I—"

Paulo interrupted again, "Yes, I am familiar with this man."

Robert got to the point, "Do you have a computer there? I want to send you a picture of a man," he paused for dramatic effect, "We strongly think it's the Shellfish Saint. Do you think you could recognize the man who proposed with the lobster?"

"No. We do not have a computer here at restaurant. Yes. I will never forget his face."

Damn. No computer.

"We do have a fax machine, though."

Robert laughed out loud into the phone. *Chuck, I love you.* He cleared his throat, "Great, can I get your fax number? I'll fax it over right now. I'm in a bit of a rush here, Paulo."

"No problem. I understand. Fax to me this photo."

"What is your fax number?"

"What is our fax number?" he, too, screamed in Robert's ear. He could hear someone scream five five five, seven four nine four.

"The fax number is five five five, seven four nine four."

"Great. Thank you, Paulo. I'm faxing now. Can you hold for one moment?"

"I am here. Take your time."

"Elizabeth!" now, he may have shouted in Paulo's ear. Elizabeth came running in, "Fax this to this number."

"Yes, Mr. Starnes."

"Just one moment, Paulo. We're faxing now."

"I am here. Take your time." Paulo wanted some conversation, "Nice guy this man was. He was so excited to put the ring on that lobster. We were so excited for him. But she say a no. It was a not pretty. He ran and the lobster disappeared, too. Later, I see on the news that other lobsters are disappearing, and I think this man might be the same man in your story. So, I put one and—"

Elizabeth screamed from down the hall, "It's done!"

Robert interrupted Paulo, "Paulo, you should be receiving it now."

"Hold on, Mr. Starnes. Yes the fax. It is ringing now."

Robert prayed this was the man. It had to be. CNN would let him tell this tragic story of heartbreak on national TV.

"It is coming through now." Pause. "Yes! This is the man! This is the man that was here that night! This is Mister Lobster!"

Robert jumped from his chair and cupped his hand over the phone, "Elizabeth, tell them to get the van ready." he returned to the phone, "Paulo, would you happen to know this man's name?"

"Yes. For sure it is in the reservation book at the front. Can you hold? I will tell you Mr. Lobster's name."

"No, Paulo. I'm heading to you, now. I'm going to call you back on my cell. Can you keep this phone line clear until I call you back?"

"Yes, Robert. Yes. Are we going to be on the TV?"

"Put on a clean shirt, Paulo. *You* are going to be on the TV. Find me that name and I'll call you right back." he hung up without even saying goodbye.

It was a quarter to five and there was still a lot to be done. Robert took a deep breath and then grabbed his jacket and flew out the door with his cell. Elizabeth walked quickly beside him with her note pad.

Robert spoke quickly and clearly, "Call Steven and tell him we got him. We'll be going live from The Fisherman's Shack on the pier." He pulled out his cell, "Damn! I forget the paper with Paulo's number."

"Got it," Elizabeth ran back to his office. She was efficient and quick. She screamed the numbers to him as she raced to catch back up.

Robert punched in the numbers and hit the call button. Paulo picked it up on the first ring.

"Hello, Robert Starnes, this is Paulo Squitti."

"Tell me you got a name, Paulo?"

"I have the name. The name is Danny Bolick."

Robert screamed, "Got him. Get ready, Paulo. We'll be there in ten minutes. Do you think you can tell this story on camera?"

"Yes. Mr. Starnes. I can tell to you this story on cameras."

"I'm counting on you, Paulo." he hung up and turned to Elizabeth, "Call Jeremy, and tell him we need an address on Danny Bolick. Tell him we need it now. Then, give that address to Steven and tell him not to call the police until we are in place. Got it?"

"Got it."

Robert was ten feet from the door and broke into a run, "Tell them to get that chopper in the air, in case he's a flyer!"

CHAPTER 36

DANNY WENT INTO the house and listened to see if she followed. She did. She slammed the door behind her.

"Danny, your pool is full of stolen lobsters!"

He went to the sink and looked out the window. Brad was climbing the fence and heading toward the pool. He must have been waiting till they came inside, not wanting to interrupt the fight.

Stacy lowered her voice, "I didn't come here to fight with you Danny. I came to say I'm sorry. I'm sorry I made you turn to this. Let me take a look at your foot."

Not so fast. "I said it's alright. Listen Becca, I appreciate you coming by."

She stared at him, "Did you just call me Becca? Who the hell is Becca?"

Danny partially laughed out loud. He did say Becca. He was glad he did and he couldn't wipe the smile off his face.

"I said, who is Becca?" Stacy steamed.

He decided not to get into it with her. That story was too long even though it was so brief. He played dumb, "What? Becca? Did I say Becca? I'm sorry, I haven't slept in a while." *Why are you apologizing? Don't apologize to her.*

"Danny, you don't just blurt out someone's name and then say you don't know them." The more angry she got, the more Danny loved the name Becca. It was like retribution seeing Stacy look uncomfortable. He only wished more eyes were on her at this moment.

195

Brad came crashing through the back door, "Danny! Danny, come quick!"

"Brad, what is it?" Danny turned to him.

Brad looked as if he were afraid to tell him, "Your lobster . . . she's floating upside-down."

Danny's face went blank. He stared at Brad for a moment in disbelief.

Brad yelled again, "Danny!"

Danny shook his head and ran right past Stacy. You could hardly see a limp in his run. He ran down the steps with Brad matching him step for step.

He crashed into the pool; and right there, in knee-deep water by the ladder, a lobster floated upside-down. He carefully reached in and grabbed her from under the surface. He gently turned her over. His fingers were touching the green spot he had put on the back of her.

Danny exhaled deeply. With his other hand, and without hesitation, he stuck his finger in the lobster's large claw. There was no pinch, no pain. He closed his eyes. Danny started to pull his finger away and the claw closed on his finger hard. He screamed out in pain. He screamed out in happiness.

"She's alive?" Brad asked sounding concerned.

"Yes! And this actually hurts like hell." Together, they laughed. Danny tried to shake his finger free. Stacy was standing at the door watching.

Danny suddenly looked to Brad, "Drain the pool."

Brad new exactly what he meant, "They're going home?"

Danny screamed, "They're going home!"

Brad ran to the pool house to open the drain. Stacy watched as Danny gently set her lobster on the concrete. The hard surface made her coil her tail, and she let go of his finger. He gently picked her up, "Hang in there, sweetie. We're on our way."

He took her inside and walked right past Stacy without saying a word. She said nothing, only watched him.

His cell on the counter broke the silence. It was Kenny. He would fix things with Kenny, but now wasn't the time. He picked up the phone and pushed a button to make it stop ringing, and then put it in his front pocket. He then searched for a small box for his lobster.

His phone rang again. It was Kenny. Danny shook his head and muted it again. There was a small box at the end of the bar. Stacy walked up to it, emptied it, and then handed it to Danny. They stared at each other for a moment.

His phone rang again, "Damn it." He reached in his pocket and pulled it out, "Kenny, I got to call you back."

"Don't hang up! Turn on CNN." his voice sounded devastated.

Danny looked at Stacy. She could tell something was wrong. Danny's only thought was, *Of course, she had to be here to see this.*

Without saying a word, Danny walked into the living room with his box. He sat down and turned on the TV. He punched in CNN's channel and his picture jumped out at them on the screen.

Stacy shrieked, "Oh my god, Danny." she sat down beside him. He turned up the volume.

"That's correct, Jessica," Robert's voice was in narration mode. "This photo was taken last night in Surf City. The man in the photo apparently robbed a local store there called Captain Jack's. What did he take . . . ? Lobsters. Lots of them, Jessica."

Brad came in the house eagerly, "Danny! Let's go! It's draining."

Danny and Stacy sat frozen, fixed to the television.

Brad walked in the room, "What's going on?" He saw Danny's face on the screen. He too fell silent. Danny still had the phone to his ear, but neither spoke.

"Jessica, police are now on the look-out for this man, Danny Bolick. They believe he may be injured. If you see this man, they are asking that you call the police, immediately."

"You have to get out of there, man." Kenny said flatly, through the receiver.

Danny's head spun. This was really happening, "Yeah. I'm sorry, Kenny."

"Don't be, brother." Kenny's voice was broken.

Still in a bit of shock because of what was happening, Danny said, "Thanks for calling," he hung up.

He first looked to Stacy, "You have to get out of here."

She looked surprised, "What do you mean, Danny? I'll be here for you when they come get you."

"I have to get out of here," he got up and ran to the back door.

"Danny!" she chased after him, "It's over. You have to turn yourself in!"

Brad sprinted past Stacy and ran out the backdoor behind Danny.

Danny first jumped in his truck and backed it up to the boat trailer. Brad was waiting there to lock it on. He quickly latched it on the hitch, "Done!"

Danny cranked it twice and then pulled forward. He then backed the boat all the way to the edge of the pool.

He jumped out. Brad was already in the pool gathering lobsters. The pool wasn't quite done draining, but a majority of the lobsters were already out of water and easy to catch. Danny grabbed the large containers from the night before and threw them down to him. Brad furiously loaded them into the box.

"Quick!" Danny screamed, "Hand me Mofo first."

In a swift motion, Brad picked the giant lobster out of the grocery cart, ran up the steps and handed her to Danny.

He jumped back into the pool, and handed Danny a full box. Danny stood on the wheel of the trailer and just dumped the lobsters into the back of the boat. He threw the box back down to Brad and grabbed the other one for himself. Together, as a team, they filled the boxes, one after the other.

"What's your plan?" Brad finally asked.

Danny paused and looked at him, "Not sure, man. Just need to get to the water. If they get me before then, it's over."

Stacy stepped in beside them with a box and started filling it. They didn't speak but instead shared a look. *Maybe she did understand.*

Box after box, they would each climb on the trailer tire and dump lobsters into *The Cubicle*. The last few proved to be harder to catch as they were still in shallow water.

"Get 'em, please," Danny said, and he exited the pool. He ran to his garage/pool house. On the table he grabbed his Swiss Army knife and stuck it in his pocket. His compass from his mother was also there. He stuck that in his pocket as well, although he knew where he was going. It would either be jail or the ocean. He ran back to the pool.

He stopped by the truck. Its engine sounded funny. Or was it some other sound? It seemed to be getting louder. He heard his neighbor's window open and out came Brad's father's head. "Brad you get away from him and get back here at once!"

Danny ignored him as did Brad. He ran to the edge, "How we doing?"

"Almost!"

Again, Danny heard the familiar noise just as it flew over them. He looked up and saw a white helicopter with a large blue nine painted on the side of it. Its search light was already on as the sun was starting to set.

"Gotta go, guys!" Danny screamed as he jumped in the truck.

Brad emerged from the pool and dumped the remaining lobsters into *The Cubicle*. "Go!" Before he even shut the door, Danny gassed it. He raced down the driveway and banked hard right, taking out Brad's mailbox – *The Cubicle* held tight.

Danny's thoughts were racing. He didn't get a chance to say anything to them. There was no time. A light startled him as it jumped on his hood. The helicopter was in close pursuit. He decided he had one goal tonight. Free the lobsters. Whatever else happened was out of his control. He had to free the lobsters.

CHAPTER 37

THE PIER'S END bar was pretty empty except for its usual crowd. Larry was in the middle of a joke when Paul the bartender screamed, "Be quiet!"

Danny's picture was on their TV as well. "Hey?" Larry looked confused, "Isn't that . . ."

"Ah, hell," Danny's father looked up to the TV. "They've found him out."

"Found who out?" asked Larry.

"Hell, I just found out the other day my damn self!" Wayne admitted.

Larry continued, "What's Danny's picture doing on the news?"

"Danny's the one been stealing those lobsters!" Wayne screamed.

"Turn it up!" shouted Andy. The TV screen changed to a bird's-eye view of the road. It started to zoom in, and then, *The Cubicle*, in all her glory was on the television, too. There seemed to be movement on the deck, the camera zoomed in real close.

Robert Starnes narrated, "Again, we believe that there is only one person in the vehicle, and that person *is* Danny Bolick. One would venture to guess that he's headed to the ocean. If you look closely the entire deck seems to be covered with lobsters. Ladies and gentlemen, we are looking at the self-proclaimed Shellfish Saint."

The helicopter's camera began to pull back. A short distance away was a group of cop cars with their lights flashing – in pursuit.

"Ah, no," Danny's father let out a moan.

"Wayne?" Larry wanted to say something but no words came to him.

"Ah, hell," Wayne moaned again. He started to scoot out of the stall. "He's heading for the boat ramp. He's gonna need our help. Andy, get your keys. You're driving."

"Everybody out!" The bartender screamed, "I'm coming with you." With that, four gray-haired sailors ran down the pier toward the boat dock, to await the arrival of *The Shellfish Saint.*

CHAPTER 38

THE COPS SEEMED to be keeping their distance as Danny looked in his rear view. He sped down Main Street and then turned left on Oleander Drive. It was now a straight shot to the ocean. He doubled checked his box sitting beside him. Come hell or high water, he was going to free this lobster. She was going to live to be one hundred years old and be able to go anywhere she wanted, whenever she wanted.

"Now, if you see a fish head in a metal box again, you keep clear! This is a one-time pass for you." Danny screamed to his lobster over the engine, "Don't you let those bigger ones push you around, either. You stake yourself a nice spot under a rock."

He ran a red light. The train of cars with flashing lights was getting longer. The helicopter was directly above him, tracking him.

Three blocks from the ramp, Danny realized they wouldn't just let him back the boat in. He put on his seat belt and picked the box up and put it in his lap. He was so close. "Hang on!" he screamed to all his lobsters in the back.

There was no time to think. No time to plan. There was only one thing he could do. Drive in headfirst and hope *The Cubicle* survived the impact. He came around the last corner and saw his father's truck pulled off to the side. The whole gang was there waiting for him. His dad, Larry, Andy, and even Paul the bartender were there. Danny gave a quick thought to who was watching the bar while he was out, but realized that all the customers were here too.

He gripped the steering wheel tight and pressed his duct-taped foot to the floor. He whizzed past everyone going way too fast. Danny closed his eyes just before impact. His seat belt locked tight on his shoulders as the truck hit the water. The trucks momentum took it all the way into the water. There was a loud bang and some broken glass over his shoulder.

Water gushed in the truck as Danny fought to take off his seat belt. *The box.* No longer on his lap the box was gone. The water was already up to his seat as he frantically searched for the box. It bumped up against his hand from under the seat.

With renewed vigor, Danny grabbed the box and exited the truck. He climbed on top of the hood and then up to the back. *The Cubicle* was off to one side but still attached to the truck.

The sirens arrived. Danny heard the cars stop and doors open. He threw the box up into the boat and in one motion lunged to the tip of the bow. With all his might Danny pulled himself up. He tried swinging a foot up and around but could not. He pulled up again. He was so close. The cops were bound to be right there in the water.

He felt a hand grab him. It was over. They got him. Then he heard a familiar voice, "I got you, son."

He looked down and his father was standing in the back of his truck with Larry and the others. They grabbed both his feet and pushed him up. He pulled himself into the boat.

Danny looked back over the edge and smiled to them, "Thanks, Dad."

"She's got a major gash on the starboard side son! Won't float for long!"

Danny thought about what he just said. *The Cubicle* was taking in water.

"Can you cut her free?" Danny screamed down.

"You get her started and we'll get her free!" All four of the old sailors reached into their back pockets and pulled out Swiss Army knives.

Danny picked up his box and ran to the wheel. He had to walk on the side of the boat, because the deck was completely covered with lobsters with all claws drawn to the ready. He set the box in the captain's chair shuffled the few lobsters that flew up on the elevated captain's deck, and turned the key.

"Freeze!" he heard from behind.

Danny turned his head and saw more cops than he could count with their guns drawn.

"Dad!" Danny screamed.

"Not yet!" Wayne called back.

"Now or never, Dad!" he felt a large push on the hull as the four men pushed *The Cubicle* from the truck.

"You're free!" he heard his dad scream, "You're free."

They were the greatest words he had ever heard him say. Danny throttled forward all full. *The Cubicle* jumped to life. He turned back to the truck. Larry was waving. He waved back. Cops quickly approached Danny's father and the rest. Some ran down the side of the launch ramp, chasing after *The Cubicle*.

Danny turned his back to them and headed for open ocean with the helicopter in tow.

The sun was leaving a beautiful sunset. On any other day, Danny would take his time, but *The Cubicle* was listing heavily to the right. *The Cubicle* was sinking.

He looked back to the shore. They were far away now. Danny had one thought. *Get the lobsters as far out as you can.*

He turned back toward the front. From out of nowhere a police boat was blocking his path. He swung the wheel hard right. He saw blue uniforms jumping ship as his boat bounced off the side of theirs. *Where had they come from?* This time he didn't look back. The engines started sounding funny as they were slowly filling with water.

The box! Danny looked down to the captain's chair. The box wasn't there. It had fallen with the other lobsters. He left the wheel and shuffled his feet through lobsters to get to the box, awakening fears from his childhood. He remembered going clamming with his father as a child and being bitten by a crab. His father had to carry his screaming body back into shore.

Now, here he was with claws all around him, *The Cubicle* leaned hard and the lobsters slid into his legs. He grabbed the box and stood up. He shuffled quickly back to the wheel. In the distance he saw a large, red boat approaching fast. *Coast Guard.*

Danny looked down into his cabin and for the first time was scared. It was nearly full of water. It was almost dark now; the helicopter's searchlight was spinning around his deck.

Danny put the box in his lap and sat down in the Captain's chair. The engine choked and then cut off. *It must be flooded.*

Waves started taking the bow of *The Cubicle* under the water. Danny rubbed her side, "I'm sorry, old friend."

The Coast Guard boat was now close enough to have its searchlight on Danny.

It didn't matter. They were too late. Water rushed in from the cabin. Danny had to brace himself as it rocked to the starboard side. The deck full of lobsters slid toward him, and the ocean began to wash them around.

Danny pulled his lobster from the box and brought it up to his face. "Now you remember what I told you, don't climb in any boxes to get a fish."

The Cubicle moaned loudly, "This is it!" he screamed to them. A wave hit them from the port side and flipped *The Cubicle* upside down, throwing Danny and the lobsters into the ocean.

He lost his grip on his lobster. The lights from above penetrated the water. Over a hundred lobsters shot in all directions. It was the most beautiful thing Danny had ever seen. They were free. He floated underwater as lobsters fled all around him.

He turned his head. One lobster, about the same size as his, lay floating, lifeless, and looking at him. *It looks like her.* Together they floated motionlessly in the Atlantic Ocean. Her power claw opened, and in an instant she shot backward into the deep. The whole time her eyes on his. Eyes. Thankful eyes.

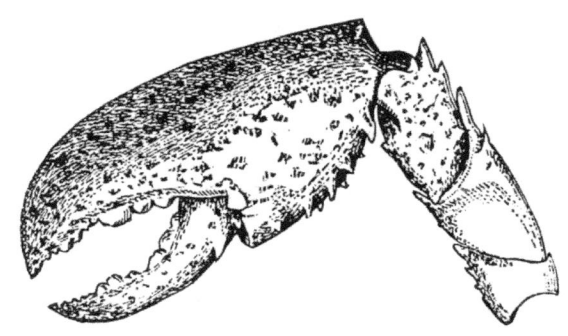

ABOUT THE AUTHOR

DAX SANTI GRADUATED from the Academy of Art University in San Francisco, with a Fine Art degree in Sculpture. He has written ever since. Don't tell his mother. He currently lives in San Francisco and continues to search for ideas to mold into stories.

www.ingramcontent.com/pod-product-compliance
Lightning Source LLC
Chambersburg PA
CBHW051504170626
46811CB00002B/649